A Man with Immense Love

Alicia Su Lozeron

Introduction

A MAN WITH IMMENSE LOVE examines the interesting character of Aiden William Melone. It portrays fascinating traits of the protagonist through the lenses of various people in his life. It depicts the differences between men and women, or on a broader spectrum, between individuals, in a complex, humorous way that brings about aspects of human existence: struggle between men and women, parents and children, as well as friends and enemies. Often, in human interactions that manifest subtle human psyches and nuances of feelings, characters and readers alike are left with a sense of catharsis that only comes about when hardships or hurtful feelings are processed and put aside to carry on with peace. One cannot help but smiling at aspects of life that so wonderfully impart wisdom or elicit awe and wonder. A Man with Immense Love is a novel that explores the topics of self-awareness, social sensitivity, and the fundamental principles of being a well-rounded and thoughtful human being.

Conveying the challenges of multifaceted dimensions in social contacts, Alicia Su Lozeron emphasizes the invaluable human capacity to self-reflect, communicate, and develop a course for living a happier life. The author aims to raise the awareness about social sensitivity, the importance of self-development into a strong and empathetic person. Her content is compelling, and her tales, beloved and beautifully narrated.

Through her communication management /travel consulting company, Asia-America Connection Society, AACS 亚美合作协会, Alicia Su Lozeron has been promoting life-long learning and global competence. Her diligence in providing quality content related to the wellbeing of the global community has proven to be rewarding, both to her own personal fulfillment, and to the global community. For herself, her work is her cause and calling. She gains a great deal of gratification through hard work and creation. For the world, her work is helpful and educational in the ways it elevates peoples and cultures of various heritages, embracing citizens of the global village, with their fair share of rights to being, to life, and to our magnificent Earth.

Alicia Su Lozeron's advocacy for mutual understanding and collaboration among individuals or cultures is vital for your company or personal accomplishments, on a business, cultural, educational, or entertainment dimension. Readers' have responded and stated that Alicia Su Lozeron's work:

• helps me overcome difficulties or fears and find beauty in positive human interactions;

• helps me appreciate people of various backgrounds, and expand knowledge about the world;

• helps me better interracial or blended family relations;

• helps me savor intricate feelings and emotions about important subjects in life;

• helps me gain enjoyment through poetic narrations;

• helps me heighten a new perspective of hope, courage, and respect for others;

• helps me raise awareness about cultural competence;

• helps me nurture a well-rounded outlook;
• motivates me to promote an open/just community;
• urges me to develop ability to see the big picture using multiple frames of references;
• helps me strengthen the ability to express genuine love;
• helps me decrease conflict by learning to trust and resolve disagreements….

"Think Global Live Noble"–together we can build a better world!

ISBN: **978-0-9981941-8-9**

Works by Alicia Su Lozeron --

The Un-death of Me: Life of an Asian American Woman
(2016, A Cross-genre "Fictional Memoir")
Asia-literacy and Global Competence: Collections and Recollections
(2017, English and Chinese Versions)
Global Competence Revisited
(2019, English and Chinese Versions)
Writings in the Time of Coronavirus
(2021, English and Chinese Versions)
A Man with Immense Love
(2022, English Version)

Upcoming --

The Un-death of Me: Life of an Asian American Woman
A Man with Immense Love
(Chinese Version; Japanese and Spanish Versions by a Team of Translators)

To a Life Larger-than-life ….

New York, Las Vegas, Los Angeles, Vancouver,
Toronto, London, Sydney

Asia-America Connection Society

A Man with Immense Love

Alicia Su Lozeron

Give a man a fish and you feed him for a day; teach a man to fish and you feed him for a lifetime.
-- Maimonides
(Spanish Philosopher 1135-1204 AD)

Content

"Don't you worry about a thing, child," said Aiden with an immensely comforting effect. Although he was not addressing her, she felt safe all the same. What could go wrong with a man who loved and solaced so? She did not know the price of marrying and spending a life with such a magnificent man. Slowly she would learn that for every successful and happy man, a grimacing woman may exist behind the scenes. She might be watching from a private lens, struggling with an innermost understanding of the man, while fighting to gain a sense of equilibrium of living under the shadow of a white-male dominated society. For whatever reason she winced, she did so almost always with devotion -- with love.

1. Righting People's Wrongs

Aiden William Melone was a stellar salesman whose aura encompassed personas of a stately man, an athlete, a jack-of-all trades, a good fellow, and a soulful musician -- not the bad-boy type that would consume you, but the make of a protector to be trusted with all your troubles and problems. Aiden made a living in sales, and his true mission was to serve all needs because he loved people, people who came across his path, friends, family, and strangers alike. He served with his congeniality, with his immense love of the world. He was the kind of man who said hello and would strike up a conversation easily, exuding confidence and comradery wherever he went, touching lives whenever he could.

But if you think Aiden was one of those sleek groomed phony salesmen whose only aim was to sell for profit, you are just being presumptuous. Aiden told it like it was. He sought to lend a helping hand to all, acquaintances and strangers alike. He had a knack for righting people's wrongs; he influenced people in positive ways. He gave advice for people's betterment. People liked Aiden.

Aiden sat in a plastic chair at LAX playing backgammon on his cellphone; he enjoyed his perfect pastime at the end of a business trip, while waiting for his flight home. Standing at 6'5", his figure emitted an impression of a piece of public art at the airport, eye-catching in a non-threatening, pleasing fashion. His disposition and physique pleased people, and by design, his wisecracks aimed to brighten up everyone's life. His mere pleasant existence, in harmony with any surroundings and walks of life, could bring endless joy and hope. He was a man of love, a man with immense love.

Next to Aiden, a baby howled when its mother, trying to restrain its frantic dancing limbs around her chest, plopped herself down on the airport chair. Relief was instantaneously budding on her face once she sat down, and she smiled as she managed to carry her baby along with her own massive stature to a rest. Red-faced with tears rolling down incessantly, the baby sensed none of the same kind of reprieve the mother felt, crying its heart out for the whole world to hear.

"What's going on with the lil' one? Why, are we hungry?" Aiden inquired seriously as if the baby had understood and could have formulated the reason why it's screaming at the top of its lungs.

The mother, a young woman with dark circles under her eyes, eyed Aiden suspiciously with question marks written on her face. "Are you talking to me? She just needs to sit down." She projected her needs for some rest onto her baby, apparently sleep-deprived and dog-tired.

"Oh, you must be very tired. But I think the baby wants to eat." Aiden observed and assured the woman he knew what's going on.

Aiden spoke with authority of a man with plenty of parenting experiences. His assertion intoned an assumption that the mother did not handle too well about her baby's needs or wants, at least not as well as he did.

Aiden gave the woman a skeptical look. He suggested that she fed her child immediately.

"Breastfeeding is much more than just providing nutrition and immunity to your baby. It is also a time for nursing, a time for comfort and nurturing. You can study and memorize each other's faces. If you talk or sing to your baby, you can build its trust and develop nonverbal communication."

"Her, it's a girl." The woman responded with the indication that she understood her baby's feelings and needs. Effecting her maternal instincts, she identified the baby's gender to Aiden, a stranger who took the liberty to call her baby "it," and to lecture to her about breast feeding.

The mother did not reject the unsolicited advice from Aiden, but willingly complied. It only took her a second of hesitation before she embarked on a trip to the breast-feeding area in the rest room. Exhausted or not, it seemed easier for her to just do what Aiden said than to stay seated in the plastic airport chair, next to the earnest Aiden.

Another minute later, the baby was happily sucking on her mom's breast. Her greedy intakes with traces of smiles on her faces proved to her mom that Aiden clearly identified the baby's needs. The baby was feeling safe after being fed; all traces of fear and distress because of all the noises from the crowds during travel disappeared. Presently she was warmed up and snugly comforted by her mother's familiar body and scent. She closed her eyes so peacefully, listening with intent, breathing to the rhythm of the heartbeats that inevitably coincided to bond herself with her child. Two hearts stroke the same cords when the mother and the child closely pressed their bodies together.

Comfort Nursing vs. Dad the Almighty

According to Aiden, comfort nursing was exactly what his wife Charlotte Lewis Melone was not able to provide. When it concerned his children, her stepchildren, there was no comfort to speak of. For the pair of precious children, Vera Davis and George Melone, "non-nutritive parental exchanges" were just what's required for them to bond with anyone besides their biological mother. For Charlotte, weaning the "grown" kids off the proverbial pacifiers, on the other hand, formed her principles of "tough love," albeit a constant source of conflict with her husband Aiden Melone, who overindulged his children to such an e extent that it's akin to pure obsession.

Charlotte had not adopted the "tough love principles" when she first met Aiden's children. She had been the eager one. She had been "too nice," "too goody-shoeing" and "too naïve" about loving her step-kids. When she married Aiden, she would do anything to help Aiden and please his kids.

"This bike gear will protect you. Check these pants out," said Charlotte who often took George on shopping sprees during the initial stage of their step-mom-and-stepson relationship.

"They're too dull. Can we find something cool?" George had a propensity for colorful biking pants, or everything bright and vibrant for that matter. His proclivity to grab anything shiny and flamboyant did not fade away when he grew old enough to be considered an adult. As Aiden had recounted, at three years of age, George had transported a full bucket of multihued marble balls into his toy room, and accidentally fell on those luminous rolling objects to give himself a permanent scar on the right side of his skull.

“Ok, how about these?” Charlotte enjoyed buying things and cooking for George, but she never seemed to be able to delight him or satisfy his materialistic needs or demands.

“I want these.” George held up a price tag that said “$580 USD” and assumed an air of importance. To him, “expensive name brands” unequivocally constructed prominence and magnitude of a life with value and worth.

“Ok then, we will take them.”

“Don’t tell Dad that you buy these for me. He will kill me.”

Amused, Charlotte questioned: “Why do you think he will kill you?” She was sensing George’s conflicted feelings. His desire for wealth, and for fame later in his adulthood, would often contradict Charlotte’s value system, not that wealth or fame was wrong in any shape or form, but how it essentially drove the boy to focus on the superficial levels of life -- all vanity and fanfare.

“Don’t tell Dad. Alright?” George requested; Charlotte paid for the gear.

She smiled knowingly, remembering the numerous times she failed to offer him what he thought was the best in the world.

"Why does this bou…boullaas have so many things in it?" George's face writhed as he struggled to pronounce the word "bouillaisse," pushing away his entire dinner toward Aiden.

"What don't you like, Homeslice? The clams? I will take them out for you." Aiden proposed a solution.

"It's too 'rich'! Mom will never feed me this." George elicited his biological mother's cooking as his defense and excuse so that he complained about any dinner Charlotte made.

Of course, Cina Miller, Aiden's ex-wife, had to be constantly brought up as it would simply diminish Charlotte's existence when George mentioned his mom. Charlotte could never win or gain any kindness from Aiden's children. Charlotte was just somebody who cooked for George while he lived with his Dad (in Charlotte's house), somebody who strangely substituted for the "real Mrs. Melone" to be in Dad's life all of a sudden.

"I will make banana crepes for you instead." Charlotte suggested.

"Mom makes pancakes! Not 'crepe'!" George protested.

"You eat your dinner, please," implored Aiden, trying to ease the tense atmosphere.

"I will eat pancakes if you make them." George addressed his dad, avoiding eye contact with Charlotte.

"I will give you my corn-on-the-cob. Now eat the extra vegetables, and you will be fine. I will make pancakes for breakfast tomorrow." Aiden recognized George's manipulative tactics to get away with dissert-only meals; he insisted on "healthy and nutritious" foods for his son. He spoke firmly to Charlotte:

"Please don't give him sweet stuff for dinner. He needs to learn to eat regular meals."

Or rather, Charlotte needed to learn to cook "regular meals," not elaborate dishes unheard of by young George. Two birds in one stone, Aiden corrected Charlotte's cooking recipes, and righted George's eating habits.

Whatever courses of actions or intentions with love Charlotte had exercised to win over Aiden's kids proved to be failing and agonizing. She then, started to disapprove his children and resent all three of them. She turned into this person who Aiden declared needed to learn about "comfort nursing." She felt frustrated and even disturbed knowing how entitled and invasive Aiden's kids were. She refused to cook for George after he turned eighteen and moved out of her house, on holidays or any other days. She objected to spending money to satisfy his vain pursuits. She felt a sense of repulsion like having thousands of bacteria eating away the sustenance of her entire body and making her sick with queasiness whenever Aiden's children had one of their ever-so-often "emergencies." She was aghast whenever Vera, Aiden's daughter, George's older sister, announced an array of new missions for her father to complete remotely for her life to function, more comfortably in her own estimation.

Aiden, on the other hand, continued his immense love for all people, and sought to help and guide whenever and however he could -- especially his children.

"There are ants all over my sink! What do I do?" George, at age 25, always sounded like 3, nearly whiny with panic as if the sky had fallen when he called his father for help on the phone.

"You clean the sink, put Lysol in, and let it soak for a while." Aiden was George's absolute source of support and help, his means of rectifying any wrongs in his life.

Vera remote-controlled her dad; her entitlement did not become lessened just because her dad lived two thousand miles away. She could have her father's full attention by simply describing in detail how her grandparents, her mom, and her husband's family were helping her do this and that. Aiden would jump in to make sure he was part of her life, her support group. Aiden would "show up" just to please his daughter on each and very little occasion she deemed significant: from an acquisition of a new pet, an installation of a new heater, a decision to change her employment, to a discussion of her vacation plans, an actual wedding ceremony, and then every drama she managed to conjure up in her married daily life.

"What do I do with my car, Dad? It's making funny noises in the front." Vera called long distance to reach her father for car issues, while her husband sat next to her, with no clues whatsoever about mechanics of cars or anything related to household repairs.

"I don't know. Why is your car making noises? Take a video and send it to me." Aiden dropped everything he was doing to answer every request Vera made of him, feeling proud as an all-knowing, loving father.

"Ok here we go. What do you think?" Vera came back on the phone after twenty minutes.

Aiden watched the video she sent, and concluded that it was something very simple:

"Ok, drive your car to your grandfather's. He has the tools to adjust and tighten the pulley." Vera lived in Aiden's hometown, where her grandpa still resided.

"I drive to Grandpa's, and Grandpa will know what to do?"

"Yes, show him the video you sent me. He will know what's wrong."

Aiden was an expert in everything: breast-feeding, cleaning, insect killing, car fixing, network building, business optimizing, house repairing, machine refurbishing, fast-meal preparing, career consulting, entertainment planning, party organizing, music and sports coaching, money lending, necessities supplying, and girlfriend-boyfriend-problem solving.

To offer her two cents, Charlotte chimed in and agreed with Aiden while he taught George about money management. They explained the virtue of frugality to the name-brand devotee, the young and vain George at the age of 25.

"Where do you get this shirt? It looks real cool, Dad!" George typically envied Aiden's wardrobe which Charlotte developed into a classy show case. Her economic and smart shopping made Aiden look sharp without spending a fortune.

"Charlotte bought it for me. Why, do you want one, too?"

"How much is it?"

"You know Charlotte, the expert in scoring unbelievable deals. She probably got it on sale."

"No, I'm fine. I will get my Diesel's through modeling for the company." George liked to show off his ability to get name-brands free of charge.

Aiden and Charlotte's money was spent mostly on necessities, whereas expenses on George and Vera always required them to step somewhere out of their comfort zone to meet the children's wants.

Aiden did things and bought things for "the kids" whenever and wherever their desires required. He advised his children of every single detail in their lives. He helped them with big and small decisions in their lives. He was Dad the Superhero, the Almighty, coupled with the intelligence of the genius Da Vinci.

As a matter of fact, Aiden not only helped his children but assisted neighbors, friends, relatives, and strangers alike.

"Come quickly. Two birds flew into my house. My kids are scared." Brenda Goodman, a young mother from the neighborhood came knocking on Aiden and Charlotte's door. All distressed and helpless, she added:

"My husband is not home from work yet. Can you help?"

Aiden successfully shooed away the pigeons out of the neighbor's window. Ever since then, he frequently brought candies and goodies for Brenda's kids to show neighborly love. The kids loved him dearly, always shouting "Hi, Aiden" miles away whenever they saw him in the neighborhood. They loved Aiden as if he had been their own flesh and blood, their Uncle Aiden.

"Uncle Aiden! Uncle Aiden! Come look; we got a new puppy," yelled Brenda's kids out of their bedroom window.

"Uncle Aiden! How are you today? We're going to take a walk." Those kids could not help but report every little detail of their lives to their beloved Uncle Aiden.

On one occasion, Aiden's college buddy Jay Robinson called up to chat about his life condition:

"Hey, dude. How are you? Still playing guitar every single day? I've got this fantastic Gibson Les Paul traditional model. It plays beautifully, man!"

"Good to hear you're still jammin' like you used to. I happen to have a 100th anniversary SG sister model. Together, they'd make a gorgeous pair, I'm tellin' you." Aiden was all stoked up hearing about the instrument he loved the most.

"What? Do you want to buy mine?" Jay was notorious for pawning his belongings for booze and drug money.

"Are you selling?"

"Nah, I am keeping this one in the family. Gonna pass this one down."

"Good. Don't sell it to the pawn shop for cheap. Keep it in the family." Aiden encouraged.

One week later, Jay phoned again:

"Hey, Buddy, did you want to buy my Gibson to make a pair with yours?"

Knowing Jay was probably having another round of his withdrawals and needing cash badly to subdue the ache, Aiden accepted the deal right on the spot. He said without a bit of hesitation or doubt:

"Jay, you need to deal with your substance-abuse problems once and for all. I'll buy the guitar to help you -- not to have money to drink or get high, but to have means to join an AA to start over somehow…."

Les Paul was shipped to Aiden, and Jay went on to procure whatever the amount of "remedy" the money enabled him to get.

On another occasion, Aiden's cousin-in-law also called for help:

"Don't tell my husband my fridge is broken. He will have a fit." Grace Joes begged.

"What happened?" Aiden was sincerely concerned.

"The fridge just quit working in this hot weather. Please come take a look so it won't cost your cousin an arm and a leg."

"I will be on my way." Aiden gladly complied without any reservation.

Aiden was an aide on demand for Grace. One day Charlotte and Aiden were about to leave for a planned dinner while Grace had another crisis:

"My BMW was leaking oil of some sort. Can you come take a look before that brother of yours decides to get rid of my old baby car?"

"We are meeting some friends for dinner this evening. Can it wait?" Aiden inquired patiently.

"No, I am going out too. It's not safe to drive across town, right?"

"Ok, we can take a detour to your house before we go to dinner. Sit on tight. We'll be right over."

Charlotte rushed to ready herself for a visit with Grace and for a dinner with friends. The pursuits of Charlottes' daily life were put on hold, just so she could be dragged around with Aiden to solve other people's problems. For some reason, Aiden insisted for Charlotte to accompany him on those rescue missions, as if with Charlotte around, those interruptions of their own daily life had become legitimate and vindicated. Eventually, Charlotte refused to run around like a headless chicken for others. She was determined to prioritize her own life over others'. And so, she let Aiden go about helping others by himself. She gave up trying to make him understand that her own needs or their life together was just as important as accommodating others.

Aiden's goodness and ingenuity had no limit, expanding to his employers, and his networks of business associates. Aiden could do no wrong. In fact, he seemed to be always righting people's wrongs.

"You think dressing like a millionaire will help sell your products. No, the opposite. I dress like I make an honest living. No fancy name brands. No excess."

He explained further and pointed out the benefits of being an "honest dresser."

"That's why my wife Charlotte and I get along. She is a woman of substance. No superficial show-offs or hot airs."

He even provided his expert opinions on optimization of company operations.

"There ought to be first-class product development to go with our outstanding sales team. I mean, how can we sell if our products always have problems?"

"Marketing doesn't do enough. I google the industry and our company does not even pop up. It's a joke for a big company like ours."

"My wife is a marketing content writer. Her company provides marketing services on all platforms. Why don't we consult some marketing firm specialized in our industry? I am sure there's got to be experts in our line of work that can help us reach goals!"

Aiden's expertise oftentimes embodied a display of impatience toward others' incompetence or unwariness. Shouting at a moving car, he frantically gestured to the driver:

"You've got a flat tire! Slow down, slow down! Buddy!"

"You need to move over to the slow lane. You're driving too slow and it's dangerous for others! For God's sake, why are you driving 45 miles per hour on a highway?"

"Don't you know how to drive, woman? Signal! Come on, signals are required here."

He barked at other drivers on the road, as if they had heard him unmistakably in their own blaring moving vehicles. Charlotte, who sat next to Aiden in the passenger seat, was the only person who heard and had to listen to his road-rage rants. He urged others to improve their driving skills -- even when his advice was delivered in a way it's audible only to Charlotte.

"What kind of driver is that? Come on, Buddy. Don't you see I am letting you in. You can't even signal. Seriously, are you just going to cut in front and then slow down? How asinine!" Red with rage, Aiden burst into a litany of complaints sonorous enough for the world to hear, though again, his tirades were only audible to Charlotte who sat next to him in the passenger seat.

Aiden also complained about modern cars, explaining what cars used to be like and how car manufacturing should have developed.

"I think there's a conspiracy among car designers and manufactures. They make things hidden and complicated, so that you cannot fix your own cars anymore. You have to take them to the car dealers."

"An igniter should be plain in sight. Older cars all had them right there in front of you." He further specified. He was bound to expose rich corporations' schemes and to advise the whole world of how cars should have been manufactured.

Aiden also showed expertise in holistic approaches to healthy living. He was conscious of sustainable methods of world development:

"Processed food is no good for you, not good for the earth."

"This steak is raw but dark. It must have been frozen -- too lousy to be served on a dining table."

"Humans need meat and sugar. Since the ancient times, animals have shown an instinct of seeking what they needed to survive. There's no point in becoming a vegan or vegetarian just to show that you're conscious about your own health and wellbeing."

Meanwhile, Aiden would not go to a dentist for all he cared, even though he had lost all his molars and could not chew hard food, due to close combats during numerous hockey or football games in his youth.

He used artificial glue to solidify his own gum inside his mouth; he refused to ever face surgeries for fear of needles injecting anesthesia into his body. His low tolerance of pain caused by dentists or doctors contradicted considerably with the immensity of his lenience in the name of love. The mercy Aiden allowed for his loved ones often came with steep costs, it seemed.

2. In the Name of Love

Aiden had come home from a business trip finding his wife in bed with a couple from the neighborhood, all three of them drunk and high. He had intoned in a forcefully calmed voice only to let out a tremor exposing his uncontrollable agitation:

"What's going on here?"

"Nothing is going on here. Just having fun while you're away from home."

Nobody but Aiden's ex-wife Cina had muttered something to acknowledge his presence. And, the nearly unconscious couple had risen from the dead, stumbled, and managed to flee the scene without providing any further explanation.

Since that night, shame and grief had made Aiden resort to singing blues instead of playing his usual rock-and-roll tunes on his guitar:

"I don't need... you're giving me some help, some help I don't really need." He closed his eyes tightly as he sang. Even presently, many years after his ex-wife became his ex-wife, he would croon B.B. King's every now and then.

In the name of love, Aiden had tried to keep his family together for as long as he could have managed to.

"Why is Daddy not sleeping in the master bedroom?" Young Vera had not been old enough to discern the facts that her mom Cina had been bi-sexual and sleeping around with friends and enemies alike.

"Daddy is just too exhausted and needs to have a night of peace." Aiden had whispered softly to his young and innocent daughter, a knot forming in his throat.

"Vera is coming to help daddy!" She had always loved to snuggle with Aiden, and the grown version of her continued to look for her father's pajamas to wear whenever she came to visit Aiden and Charlotte.

"How is Vera going to help Daddy?" Aiden had inquired, feigning curiosity even though he had been aware that his little daughter had wanted to accompany him and proclaimed her company to be the solution of every problem in Aiden's life.

George on the other hand, had not been as big of a help as Vera. He had always added to Aiden's trouble:

"Daddy, George wants to play outside." He had needed another good pair of running shoes, paints, gloves, glasses, or hockey sticks or speakers or something else. The list never ended or stopped growing as time passed.

George's and Vera's senses of entitlement to everything Aiden owned, the entirety of Aiden's existence, were immeasurable. They not only devoured on the emotional level, but also materialistically. Aiden was embracing all their needs; he had no telling as to which one of those demands, wants, and desires would consume more of him. He only knew to hold on to those two kids and gave them whatever they wanted, because deep down, he knew they were losing their most precious thing in life: the way of only an intact family could offer, with their biological mom and dad working together to make sense of their worlds.

Aiden had worked hard to provide and satisfy his family's needs. The kids had only understood that their mom had been having issues with "a glass of drink or two," and had been having a hard time keeping up with her spirits. Cina was all giddy one moment, and the next thing you know, she was a different animal, tossing and smashing all the plates in the cupboard onto the floor for all the clanking and cracking to muffle the "noises" inside her head.

"Why do I have all the meals to cook, dishes to load and laundries to fold all the god damned time? I don't want all these plates!" The precious China had turned out to function like mufflers to soften Cina's cries and shrieks as she made furious and desperate gestures, sweeping away all content inside the cupboard onto the wall and the floorboard.

"Mom, are you OK? Should I call an ambulance for you?" At a young age, Vera had taken on an adultlike composure.

"Nobody…uh…uh…needs…a damned-damned…ambulance. I need to have uh. .. some parties...noises...." Cina yelped with intermittent hiccups and burps.

Aiden had rescued Vera and George from the coat closet that night and taken them to rent an apartment from Bruce Chen in downtown. The kids named that period of their life "the Bruce Chen Years," happily training under the Kung Fu master from the Far East.

"I am riding a bicycle with Bruce Chen today. He said it's part of the training." George had exclaimed.

"Be careful not to ride on the streets too much. Go to the park." Aiden had been as protective as ever, and George, as daring as he would turn out to be:

"I am going to be a Kung Fu superstar!"

On the brink of his divorce from Cina, Aiden had to make a choice: to take Vera or George to move to the East Coast for his job. He had taken Vera.

George had stayed with Cina, and consumed chicken nuggets while growing up to be the pickiest eater in the world, skinny but naturally athletic. Vera had moved to the East Coast with Aiden; she learned to speak vivaciously with wild gestures like an ever-energetic mini-Aiden. The two kids grew to be very different people, but they were as tight as two peas in a pod when defending the honor of their biological mother, Cina. There was something about blood family that one could not take away or eliminate however one might try or wish. The bond between the mom and her children was intact. Cina's promiscuity, or mental and drinking issues, had ended her marriage with Aiden. But Cina remained Vera and George's favorite woman in the entire world; no one could compete with Cina.

In fact, no one could take Aiden away from Cina as far as her children were concerned. She was the only Mrs. Melone. Charlotte, Aiden's second wife, was the "fake" Mrs. Melone, not completely accepted to the Melone family, at times treated worse than a stranger, with antagonism, malice, and hatred.

Charlotte resented how uncomfortable she was made to feel around Aiden's kids.

"Are we going out? What is the plan?" Charlotte inquired at her dining table full of dishes she made for Vera when she came to visit occasionally after she reached adulthood and was married to a fellow from her hometown.

"Um…" Vera did not reply, responding with a guttural sound from her throat. She was in grave pain simply because Charlotte was sitting at the same dining table.

In general, Vera avoided Charlotte and demanded Aiden's full attention and assistance with all aspects of her life.

"Daaaaaaaad.... We need to talk about my car. Why is it squealing when I brake? Where should I take it to be fixed? Can you do it for free, Dad?" Vera gave Aiden a stare with her eyes rolling to one side and mouth slanted mischievously. Her looks told Aiden: "I am the most important person in your life. No one else matters. No one else counts."

"Daaaaaad! I need to borrow a warm jacket and your truck early tomorrow morning. Mandy and I are going rock climbing." Vera often took her friends along with her when she came to visit "her Dad's house," meaning Aiden and Charlotte's residence which Charlotte had purchased before she married Aiden.

"Daaaaaad! Mandy doesn't eat meat. Can you make some vegetarian dishes?" She addressed Aiden even though Charlotte was the one cooking.

"Daaaaaad! You need to take me to the theater tonight."

"Daaaaaad! You need to pay for Brandon and me next time we come visit. We want a staycation as a 2nd honeymoon present!"

"Daaaaaad! You should buy me a fancy dress for my party."

"Daaaaaad! You need to make better cakes. Not so much sugar!"

"Daaaaaad! Brandon and I expect to get a brand-new Tesla as our anniversary present. Get to it!"

"Daaaaaad! You need to go pick up my friend Shelly."

"Daaaaaad! You need to make things right when your daughter comes to visit."

"Daaaaaad!"

"Daaaaaad!"

"Daaaaaad!"

Dumbfounded by Vera's sense of entitlement and never-ending demands, Charlotte looked at Aiden helplessly. Aiden took his wife aside and whispered to her ear:

"I am so glad I don't have kids home anymore. Be careful what you wish for. Don't tell me you want more kids."

Aiden's kindness, his immense love for the world, encompassed a need he himself did not realize -- an everlasting need to please his children, his friends and family members. Aiden's good nature also embodied a survival instinct that was converted into a refusal to bear any kids with Charlotte.

Charlotte always wanted to have her own biological children with Aiden. It was Aiden who had done enough of the parenting; he feared the prospect of having more kids. When they were younger, Charlotte had a hard time accepting the fact. Now Charlotte went along with it and was thankful for not adding more challenges of raising kids in their family.

Aiden had paid dearly for the loss of the bond with his children's biological mother. His leniency toward the loved ones had not saved his first marriage. His permissiveness would not prepare his children for the changes in their lives, either. Aiden wanted to protect everyone, and he ended up sidestepping, giving too much and at the same time, not enough. And perhaps, only with compassion and patience, his life with Charlotte, with or without his children, could amount to a certain level of existential bliss, something akin to acceptance and thoughtfulness.

In the name of love, Aiden was locked in a cage for the longest time; his children would not let go and grant him any right to happiness. Like a bird with its wings trimmed and shaped to satisfy its owner's esthetic or pragmatic purposes, Aiden was restrained and could not fly away.

In the name of love, Aiden justified his everyday life with Charlotte in a manner that put her in the same cage with him. Old strings and new cords of a web of emotional baggage intertwined in such a way that they blocked their visions and blinded them; they could not see their priorities or orders of things clearly. What their love and life together could bequeath was not unblemished. Jointly, their journey required more of freedom and autonomy -- more of the merriment that only exists with a sense of equilibrium -- for all parties involved.

3. A Sociable Person

Aiden was gregarious and needed people around him. He liked to call every relative and close friend on the weekends:

"Hey Brother, how're you doing? It's Aidee calling from the magnificent East Coast."

"Hey, I'm fine. What're you up to?" Aiden's older brother Trent Melone always showed his brotherly love whenever Aiden called him up.

"Nothing much, just about to watch a movie with my lovely wife. What's going on with you?"

"We have a house full of kids and grandkids again. The lil' ones are just lovely." Trent had 11 grandchildren at the age of 60.

"Oh, isn't that wonderful," said Aiden with envy.

"Hello, how are you feeling?" Aiden called up his older sister often.

Suffering from chronic pain, Susie Melone minimized her sufferings and anguishes by imagining a life without travails or woes in her own mind. She had the habit of understating what's going on in her life:

"I am just fine."

"Any results back about the MRI, X-Ray, or CAT?" Aiden asked with great concern.

"Yes, nothing major on the report."

"What did the doctor say?"

"Just that I need to rest more."

"Then, don't kill yourself working so hard. Have Ken help you with the business more." Aiden suggested.

"I will." Susie was running a restaurant supply distribution business, and her terse answers to Aiden effected efficiency. Efficiency both on the business and the home fronts. No small talks.

"Take care of yourself. I love you." Aiden expressed his affection.

"Love you, too. Bye."

Aiden not only wanted to call his siblings on the phone, but sought all opportunities to meet up with them.

"Let's make time this summer to see Yellowstone." Charlotte had wanted to see the national park for a long time.

"Ok. Let me round up my brothers and sisters. Let's see if they can meet us up there somewhere close."

For Charlotte, a trip or vacation was a learning process, a mean to regain equilibrium; for Aiden, it's better with family and friends, another gathering and fun event packed with people, any family or friends who happened to be in proximity.

When Aiden called up his best friend Peter Young, he always had a lot to chat about:

"Hey, Pete. Howdy-do? Did you watch the game yesterday? Isn't that something? They turned it around in the last minute!" Aiden liked to discuss hockey, football, golf, basketball, baseball and all other games and sports with his college buddies.

"Tell me about it, right? Man, what a beautiful shot!"

"I can't say that their defense was all that perfect, though." Every little detail, strategy, movement in a game concerned Aiden.

"Well, in the end, it all worked out for them. I watched it with Jay, Calvin, Monk, and Toothie last night. We had a blast!"

Most of Aiden's buddies still lived in his hometown in the north. Aiden always got nostalgic on the weekends, and had to call them to check their weather, their morale, their girlfriends, wives, children, jobs, and all that's happening in their lives. On top of that, he got to gab about sports, current events, and the world's funnies and miseries.

Aiden always ended up talking about his own kids, making sure to have a good laugh. Charlotte sometimes felt utterly detached and would engage herself in a completely different pursuits than Aiden on the weekends, cooking, shopping, reading, writing, playing the Uke she loved, or going for a spa day with her friends.

When Aiden chatted with his kids, he demonstrated another level of persistence in being sociable. He made calls to his children about 5 times a day. As a matter of fact, George called up Aiden twenty times a day to say hello, ask for advice, or drag Aiden to have a one-on-one session somewhere outside the house without Charlotte. It was a great way to get Aiden to buy him a meal, treat him to some special event, and have Aiden run more errands on his behalf or solve more problems in his melodramatic life.

"Hey Dad, I need to renew my subscription for SoundData. Is it better to go for two years for $300, or $20 a month?" He wanted to know whether the service was essential for his music career.

"Well, do you use it all the time? Do you need it for long-term?" Aiden taught George how to manage his job expenses -- and everything else in life.

"Hey Dad, I need to ask you about the trip to Chicago. This club is paying for my expenses to go DJ there, but I won't get any additional pay. Should I take it?"

"Well, exposure is always good. Do you think there's potential to explore other opportunities like producing and recording through this trip?" Aiden coached George about capitalizing on business prospects.

"Hey Dad, I need to have a break from Jennie. She's having another episode."

"Well, what did I tell you? She's too unstable. You need to think about your life." Aiden advised George on girlfriend issues, courtships, friendships, and relationships. George continued to have his offs-and-ons, ups and downs with Jennie, and other different girlfriends at various stages of his love life.

"Hey Dad, we have a hockey game tonight. What time are you showing up?"

"The game starts at 8:00. I'll be there at 7:00." Aiden couldn't wait to get to the game with his son.

"Hey Dad, can I borrow that Martin guitar and that chili-red strap of yours? I have a performance tonight."

"Well, you can borrow the guitar. Don't be so cheap; buy your own strap!" Aiden declared jokingly.

"Hey Dad, I need you to change the guitar strings for me on my Seagull."

"No problem. Come on over. I have strings for you that will last a lifetime."

"Hey Dad, my toilet is plugged. Can you come over to fix it?"

"I am at work, son."

"Can I borrow your plunger then?"

"Yes, come over to the house and get it."

"Hey Dad, I am stock on the roadside. I need your help! Can you come over to pull me out the dirt pile?"

"I am in bed already, son."

"Who else can I call?"

"Yes, I will get up and come right over."

"Hey Dad, I just pooped my paints. It's stormy outside!"

"I don't know what to do about that."

"Can you tug me in?"

"Just go to bed. You'll be all right, son."

Aiden and Charlotte's house stored all the tools and necessities for all George's maintenance and repair needs. Yes, he would come for a plunger, or – ah, a piece of printing paper.

When Aiden called up his children, he was especially sociable:

“Whaaaat up? Handsome.”

“Heeey, Homeslice, where did you get those shirts you’re selling online?”

“Top of morning to you, Sweetie.”

“How’re you doing today, Honey.”

“Hello! Are you going to the game today, Dude?”

“Heey, come over now; let’s have a chat about your upcoming gig, Brother.”

Aiden would seek Vera’s praises for all the good deeds he engaged in to better her life from a distance. He would summon George to the house to help him with whatever without informing Charlotte what they were doing. Charlotte would have to be always ready for George’s announced or unannounced visits. Oftentimes, she just closed the door of her study, and buried herself in work, or busied herself with her own pastime. A door closed is a boundary set. No one can violate that.

And yes, Vera, though living in a different city, was predisposed to call up Aiden on unexpected hours, especially when Charlotte and Aiden were in bed watching TV or reading side by side. She could wait to call during more "sensible" hours for recipes, discussions about life or politics, car issues, or missions for her dad to complete. But she always chose to call and take up hours of her father's time. Vera was more important than anything or everyone else, only in rivalry with her own brother.

Neither Vera nor George would ask to say hello to Charlotte who was lying right next to Aiden during the calls. Rarely would Aiden remember to engage Charlotte and the children to any level of connection. He was afraid of rocking the boat. It was easier to just let things develop in their own courses. In Charlotte's mind, it was just as simple to stay at a distance, so that she would not be hurt in the awkward family dynamics over and over again.

To those children, Charlotte was invisible, non-present and non-tangible like some artifact buried in a tomb -- you would have to dig and search to be sure of its existence. Aiden was too occupied with being a "great" father to risk his bonds with the kids by inserting Charlotte into their lives. Nothing was more important than keeping those two kids happy and close to him. When people loved him -- especially so long as his children adored him, Aiden felt content and terrific about life.

Charlotte understood that Vera and George might avoid her intentionally, on the phone or face-to-face – just as she avoided them. What she had a hard time accepting was how Aiden could overlook way too often, the opportunities to facilitate better and fairer vibes. Aiden never once urged his children to celebrate Charlotte's and his own wedding anniversary, or anything related to Charlotte. Quite contrarily, he expected Charlotte to buy presents or recognize his kids' birthdays, graduations, dating anniversaries, holidays, or other occasions that were significant according to them. There was no balance in the give-and-take, and it further enabled Vera and George to feel entitled. Aiden's condolence for the children's rudeness toward Charlotte made Charlotte writhe with anguish and sadness. She rebelled against becoming a benefactor for unkind recipients of good will. She did not believe in the Christian doctrine of offering her other cheek for slapping after being slapped on one check. For her, prayers for the unkind only permit more wickedness. Her aversion or animosity was only augmented. Without a fair game of exchange or mutual respect, there was never any relationship to speak of. In the end, any gesture of kindness or courtesy disappeared into thin air, frozen in mid-action in her subconsciousness, forever incomplete, altered, and distorted. It would take her own demise for her to be with Jesus again.

Women are generally more social than men. They have the knack of connecting with people and arranging social affairs, packing days with plans and activities. But it was quite the opposite for Aiden and Charlotte. She would organize events that she thought were worth investing time in, or she would find things to do together with Aiden for his sociability to have an outlet of some sort. Aiden craved constant human contact, as if his whole existence had depended on such dealings with people.

Charlotte once gathered people together in their house to celebrate Aiden's birthday. You must agree that women tend to do things to please their men, while men think about pleasing the whole world. Knowing that social approval made Aiden tick, Charlotte summoned up her gusto on the phone: "Are you coming this Sunday? We certainly enjoy your company!" All invitees showed up for Aiden, jammed in their house for the celebration.

"Why, Aiden is looking superb for his age!" Dian was quite fond of Aiden and often expressed her admiration publicly.

In contrast, Dian's husband Danny would openly argue with Aiden about everything and anything under the sun: "So what do you say about the proposal to rid America of private health care? You really agree killing thousands of jobs is the answer?" He fumed with excessive indignation.

"Something's got to be done. I know universal healthcare works."

"It doesn't make sense to take away many people's jobs to support a system that we don't know will work in the States or not."

Aiden countered with confidence: "When you can address the problem of having M-O-N-E-Y determine everything in this country, the answer is yes. The system will work out." Spelling out the underlying trouble of our society made Aiden feel just as dignified.

"How can you justify taking away people's means of making a living?"

"If it's honest living, sure, we can have the options of private insurances plus government regulations. It's when you don't provide healthcare but focus on monetary pursuit, things become crooked."

"You're simplifying the situation. Why do you think we have to sacrifice to take care of the poor or the uncared for?"

"It's not only about the poor, its' about human rights. Even when you're covered in America, you still risk your entire fortune in your old age for unforeseen diseases or health issues. Nobody should have to pay $5000 deductibles before receiving healthcare."

Danny would not give in: "America's got the best doctors. And good healthcare costs money. Why do you think people come here to have major surgeries or treatments?"

Aiden saw no point of continuing the discussion and decided to lighten up the atmosphere: "Why don't I sing a few songs to make you happy?"

While we were young
We used to sing by the apple tree
We sang shalalala lalalala lalala
We sang dudulelu dudelu delulu
We were young and cheery….

Playing the guitar, he sang his favorite tunes. People started to gather and circle around him, applauding and cheering. Fueled by others' compliments, Aiden sang for 2 hours straight without any sign of fatigue. He looked very energized and youthful.

"Sing some songs you composed yourself, Aiden," suggested Kevin who dabbled in songwriting and pursued a stardom persistently into his middle-aged years.

"Ok, here we go."

When I call you don't shy away
I just want to get to know you
Baby nobody makes me feel this way
You make me feel young again

When I see you don't look away
I just want to team up with you
Baby nobody makes me feel this way
You make me feel alive again

When I hold you don't get away
I just want to be one with you
Baby nobody makes me feel this way
You make me feel love again

When I call you don't shy away
When I see you don't look away
When I hold you don't get away

With the light-hearted rhythms of Aiden's songs, people were singing along. Aiden's fun-loving spirit was contagious. When all people around him were enthused and motivated, Aiden became the happiest person in the entire world.

Aiden liked to praise people just to make them feel warm.

"Don't you look lovely today, Ms. Miller."

"You can count on me, Buddy. A nice guy like you deserves the best."

"How lucky I am to spend such a wonderful evening with all of you fantastic people!"

Other than playing music with a bunch of people around, Aiden was always jubilant when he played hockey, golf or any sport and game.

"George and I always encourage our team members," said Aiden proudly, "and we teach them how to line up for the goal."

"Without me and George, our team could not get to the finals." Aiden added, "George is the best scoring player in the entire league."

Aiden's excitement about life in general was not free of exaggeration or amplification of his own glory.

He often announced his or his family's success or fanciful qualities.

"I just made a big deal. Half a million in commission is coming and I am going to retire soon!" Aiden had been hinting his imminent retirement since the age of forty-five.

"My boy George is a born star. So talented and handsome nobody can resist him!"

"My daughter Vera is beautiful inside out. She will go places and retire at the age of 35. Nobody can stop her!"

"My wife Charlotte is a marketing guru. Her campaigns move mountains. She is such a beautiful person, a wonderful writer to boot. I've married up really – she is way out of my league!"

For sure, Aiden was brilliant in his own ways. A lousy speller, he never felt good about English classes or writing. However, he was the one who could write fast and come up with one thousand words in thirty minutes. He could make an impromptu speech and engage his audience with his sincere words and candid spirit. He could do finances in his head and figure out how much one lost or won in the stock market in seconds. He could answer trivia questions and come up with responses quicker than many Jeopardy contestants. He truly dabbled in many fields and was equipped to provide tactics or solutions.

Aiden was an outgoing man; he was always up for anything and everything positive. No downers could get to Aiden because he's determined to live life to the fullest. He was all spunk, not a mean bone in his body -- no malice, and no nonsense.

His sociable, spunky, no-nonsense kind of business acumen propelled many people to gather and listen to him on a trade-show floor. His conference calls were full of merriments on top of strategic alliance-forming discussions and negotiations. Aiden was a successful salesman. He was an accomplished man, with lots to give.

4. His Reticence at Home

Although Aiden was always loud and talkative around people, he could be awfully taciturn and uncommunicative at times, especially when he was at home.

"What do you feel like for dinner?" Charlotte asked Aiden after a long day of work.

"...." Silence seemed to be Aiden's way of saying: "Whatever."

"We've got shrimp scampi and leftovers from the restaurant the other day. Or, I can make a fresh batch of roasted vegetables with chicken Marsala?" Charlotte was trying to gauge whether a light meal would be more to his liking that day.

"Whatever you make, honey, is fine."

Washing and cutting mushrooms, peppers, cauliflowers, broccolis and potatoes, Charlotte tried engaging Aiden in a conversation:

"How is work today? Any development on the Rendahl account?"

"I'm trying." Aiden worked hard on the deal with Rendahl for months and was close to signing the service agreement. When talking about it to everyone else, he was super excited and emphasized how much he would feel achieved with such a huge and prestigious client. Vera, on a phone conversation with Aiden, was readily making demands: "Dad, if you close this deal, remember you'll be able to buy me and Brandon a Tesla that we always wanted."

Charlotte thought to herself, listening to the conversation on the speaker phone: "It'd be nice if Aiden gets to save money for himself and is able to retire one day."

"You don't sound very excited," observed Charlotte, with a melancholy timbre in her voice. She wondered why in their private conversations about anything, Aiden's excitement never reached the same level as when he was talking to everybody else.

"Because it's not finalized."

"Just checking to see if there's any…."

"Sh…."

"Sh…sh…shh…." Aiden often shushed Charlotte when she tried to make conversations. Her intent was hushed by his reluctance to make effort to share or to engage in mental or emotional connections while he longed for a quiet time at home.

He could make Charlotte feel that he only acknowledged Charlotte's existence in the same house or in his life when he wanted something from her. That "something" when they were younger was:

"Come here, honey. I am hot for you."

"Come here, honey. Show me some love."

It turned into a different "something" as they aged:

"Where's my blue tie, honey?"

"Can you fix this zipper for me?"

"Ok, that's too much food. I can't eat any more. What's for dessert?"

Charlotte was often sequestered in a corner of Aiden's mind. Taken for granted or not, she felt the need to regain and re-center herself in her own life, in their life together. At home or at social settings, at any age of their lives, their connection or communication should not have ebbed so. With no nourishment or effort, came only stagnation and bleakness.

They say couples feel so loved and comfortable around each other: silence is gold. Aiden's reticence did indeed, implied a certain level of understanding and contentment when he was alone with Charlotte. He would show a completely different side when he was around people, especially his clients and his children. He would sing out loud "I Can Show You the World," completely enthused about Jasmin, the princess of Aladdin and telling his clients how Vera loved the story. He would pose next to the princess impersonator at a Disney-themed trade show, and have his picture taken to send to Vera. He even had Aladdin and Jasmin's picture on a magic rug painted on Charlotte's bathroom wall to show his "romantic and sensitive" side!

Charlotte was aghast to come home one day and see the cartoon figures among her collections of home décor items. The kitschy feel of the caricature made Charlotte feel defeated in her bathroom, and it deepened her sense of despondency and loneliness. Indeed, as Vera declared at family gatherings to her father:

"Who is more important than I am?!"

Vera's self-importance, George's entitlement, together with Aiden's accidental insensitivity, took away Charlotte's warmth or feeling of love toward her husband on many occasions. And, the imposition of Aiden's children in Charlotte's life, at times made her want to get away from it all, far far away.

Presently at the dinner table, which Aiden seldom occupied, Charlotte thought about the inadequacy of her own life, and how it might be viewed differently from others' perspectives:

"Come on, don't leave two bites. It's hard to keep that amount of food as leftovers." Charlotte urged Aiden to finish his dinner, as he often ate in front of TV in bed and left two bites on his plate for Charlotte to collect.

She called him Addie-Two-Bites and hoped to change his eating habit. She encouraged him to eat in the dining room. Her hopes were to please his stomach, as if it were also a way to fill his inner void -

- a remedy for not having his children living in the same household day in and day out. Aiden needed his children constantly. Grown or not, they were his delights. And Charlotte realized Aiden would always choose his kids over her, thought about them before he considered their married life together. Well, Aiden was a father first before he was Charlotte's husband, while Charlotte, a person in her own rights, before she could live for other people.

Aiden's extrovert personality required constant involvement of others' input, while Charlotte's introvert instincts drove her to look inwards at their own life together. She was content entertaining herself writing, reading, creating art, cooking, playing musical instruments, or doing whatever in her study, dining room, living room, bedroom, bathroom, or patio. Aiden, on the other hand, needed people -- his need to please and serve people conflicted with his wife's desire for a self-sufficient emotional status. His insensitivity to her entreaty for privacy or intimacy hurt her.

Charlotte could see Aiden's tendency to overlook any factor of importance for enhancing their life together if it did not help portray his own image of a champion at any given point in time. He cared for his likability and popularity more than he did for a happy wife. He did not consider Charlotte's individuality, to the extent that she would revolt and rebel.

Charlotte's protest had little effect on Aiden's behaviors or habits. He remained quiet at home, only exhibiting his gregarious personality when he felt like it. Perhaps silence is golden between a couple who are so comfortable and confident about their relationship that they do not have to be constantly conversing. But communication is always crucial for sharing and understanding of each other's needs and wants.

Charlotte needed to feel more connected with Aiden. She could not understand why Aiden often seemed cheerier when there were other people around. She could only stand up for herself, object, and plea for more consideration. Aiden would continue to listen or talk very little. Charlotte would raise hell, and at times, willfully dismantle the unity and harmony of their conjugal life.

5. I Am Marvel

I, the Marvelous George Evan Melone, was born on a Saturday in the summer; I am bound to be famous, a born star to be precise, a naturally gifted entertainer and athlete. I love music, love creating and producing beats and effects, and am always keen to help artists achieve their dreams. I have been playing with guitars, pianos, and mixers since I was three. Or, maybe five, when I started making and remixing sounds.

My father taught me everything; guitar playing and singing are his areas of expertise. I'd say I outsmart the master, becoming not only a DJ but a producer of my dad's music! My father admits that the student has surpassed the teacher. He calls me up and asks me to record and produce his songs:

"Hey Son, let's get together and put this song up."

"Anytime you can come over, you're always welcome, Dad."

Any chance I can get Dad away from my stepmom Charlotte I grab it like a piece of driftwood in the sea to help me survive and navigate the world. I feel so alone without Dad in my life every day. I am afraid of losing my way, to be honest, although I am pretty much on my own, I am still a helpless child at heart. Yes, a piece of flotsam, an unwanted person, a third wheel, is all I become, is what Charlotte makes my life out to be. I want Dad back. I hate Charlotte for taking him away from me. I hate her. I hate her guts.

Ever since my dad split with my mom, I have been searching for answers. Why did he do that? Why did he marry Charlotte so quickly after his divorce from Mom went through? Was Charlotte the reason why Dad left Mom? I think Charlotte is to blame -- for everything!

Was Charlotte the person who tore apart my family? Dad said he was already separated from Mom when he met Charlotte and Charlotte had nothing to do with his divorce from Mom. But I suspect that Charlotte had everything to do with Dad's finalizing the split! She caused it! She was the reason I became an undesirable distraction in my father's life! I should always be the Only Center for him. I should be the Only One he trusts and confides in. I should be inseparable from him every minute, every day, and all days. Why on earth would he call me a miracle of his life, nicknaming me Marvel -- if I am not the most important person in his life?!

Why did I have to come live with Dad and another woman? Wasn't I doing fine living with Mom and Vera? How would I be too messy to live with them? What troubles had I made to be sent away to live with Dad and his new wife?

In any case, I dislike everything about Charlotte, her high-paying "intellectual" type of job, her looks, her little lectures about life and change, her speeches, her actions, her thoughts, her ideas, her home décor, her cooking -- her tendency to steal my father's attention and affection. I need to win the competition with her and show her who is boss. I am Marvel!

"Me and my dad are going golfing. You don't want to go, do you? It's too hard of a sport to pick up."

"Me and my dad are making a song together. Please do not disturb."

"Me and my dad are not fond of spicy food. Can you try making good food, instead?"

"Me and my dad are playing hockey tonight. You can come watch but I don't think you understand how fast and how good I am."

"Me and my dad have to go shopping for speakers together. When we come back, I want the dinner ready."

"Me and my dad live here. I can do whatever I want to the house."

"Me and my dad have a different schedule than you. Why should I stop playing and making music at midnight?"

"Me and my dad don't need to listen to you."

"Me and my dad can jam with my friends in my studio as late as we want. We will smoke whenever and wherever we want."

"Me and my dad (though Charlotte keeps urging me to use 'proper' English saying I should always use "my father and I')…."

"Me and my dad…."

"Me and my dad…."

"Me and my dad…."

I confess that sometimes I push the limits just to see how much Charlotte would take. Other times I feel guilty for bugging her. So, once in a blue moon I would play nice for a change:

"Hanging out with my stepmom. Dude, don't come over now. She has a lot of work to do; she needs a quiet house."

"Should I turn down my music, Charlotte? Do you need me to close my studio door?"

"I will clean my room today. I know it kind of smells."

"I won't record Durvo's singing in the closet next to your bedroom, I promise. I will set up something different this time."

"Sure, you want to join me and my dad to the game?"

"My sister is visiting. Should we have a cookout together?"

"My aunt is in town. Can I go stay at her hotel for one night?"

"My aunt is giving me some money for my trip. I don't need as much pocket money this time. Thanks."

I realize that no matter how hard I try to be nicer, I am still angry with Charlotte. The loathing I feel for her seems perpetual and permanent. I know I am growing up and have to accept the fact that Charlotte is my dad's wife. But I still hate her and want to hurt her a lot of times. I am Marvel; I can do whatever I want.

I can do whatever I want – that's what Dad told me since I was born:

"You can achieve whatever you want to accomplish in life."

"You can learn to do whatever you want to do faster than anyone."

"You are natural. You are the best player on the team."

"You are a super model. GQ-style buff and all!"

"You are a star athlete. No one can beat you to it."

"You are hugely talented. You will be discovered one day."

"You can make a lot of money doing what you love to do."

"So handsome and smart, my Son."

"You are the best producer of music, and the best designer of your own life, for that matter."

Dad always encourages me and gives me advice I need every day. But everything has changed when Charlotte becomes Dad's wife. I am not the center of my dad's life anymore. He's got to take care his wify's needs and wants first before he has time for me. It's got even worse after I move out of Charlotte's house.

"Dad, can you come over to fix my garage door for me?"

"Charlotte and I are going for a gathering this afternoon. Maybe tomorrow?" There you see, he has his life to live with Charlotte.

"But my garage won't close!"

"Check and make sure there's nothing in the way of the censor that stops it from closing properly."

"Ok. So, you're not coming?"

"No, not today."

I am so pissed that Charlotte takes the front seat. Why does she have to be in the way? Why does her existence bug me so? How does she even become Mrs. Melone?!

When I lived with Dad and Charlotte, Charlotte didn't allow me to play or make music aloud after midnight.

"I couldn't sleep. Please turn off the music."

"I am almost done with this song. Another ten minutes."

"Ok, also please don't have people over late at night."

"I have to record their singing."

"Please do it during the day."

That was bull. Just because she had to get up early to work, I was to cut down all my evening activities. How was I going to make it if I couldn't have the space and time to create and produce?

I moved out when I was 18; have been on my own since. To be honest, it was nice to have all the food in the fridge whenever I felt like eating. Now, I have my own space and can make music any time I want, but I have little food in my fridge. That sucks but I get to eat the kinds of food I want and like. I have 2 roommates to share rent with, and I can have people over all the time.

No one will give me shit for the way I breathe and live, except the other day I was called in to a HOA hearing.

"We received multiple complaints that your house is always full of people and noises."

"Yes, I have a few artist clients and friends."

"When you affect the peace and quiet of this gated community, we have to take actions to set the boundaries."

"What boundaries did I violate?"

"According to the entrance records, you have too many guests. Your neighbors also reported loud partying noises last night."

"Ok, that's what I do -- making music. I understand the neighbors' concerns. I will tone down."

"This time you're getting a $1000 fine. Next time, if there's a next time -- you'll have more severe punishment."

Punishment!? As if I committed some crime! Why is the HOA person behaving like a dictator? Not fair! I swear this so called "hearing" was unjust.

The society is full of limitations and proclamations that hinder my creativity. On another hearing about hockey fights, I had to defend myself for punching back some player that pinned me down and stopped me from scoring all the time.

"He hit me first and always blocks me from scoring."

"Punching him in the face broke the rule. It's not proper hockey etiquette."

"But what was I supposed to do? He fought me first."

"You're banned from playing for a month."

That was complete nonsense too. Who doesn't fight back at a hockey game? If I don't stay competitive and aggressive, how am I going to maintain my star-player title? Good thing was that dude was also banned for a month -- otherwise I would have fought the board's decision until I saw some semblance of justice!

But don't let me digress. The thing with Charlotte is never easy. I really kind of want to like her now that I am living on my own instead of under her roof. However, I cannot show her or let her know that, especially when my sister Vera is around. Me and my sister are tight as two peas in a pod. Vera doesn't even befriend Charlotte on any social media. While I acknowledge Charlotte as my stepmom online, I refuse to do her further favors (she rarely responds to my posts, duh!). And I still hate her to my guts, though yes, sometimes I feel alright about her. At any rate, I have my music to promote online. Offline, I show my politeness to Charlotte when my dad is present to witness my good manners. Who knows? -- perhaps Charlotte will leave more of her assets to me after she passes – if I play nice. But what really gives me satisfaction is to team up with Vera to show Charlotte who's important. Who is as sleek as I am anyway? I kill it on all fronts. I am a star. I am the boss. I am Marvel.

6. The King

As a matter of the fact, Aiden was the important one, the King, admirable and influential in the circles of his family, friends, and associates. He was a big shot to his kids, siblings, neighbors, friends, coworkers, enemies, and clients. He liked to be big, he felt that he was smarter than anyone he knew, and he commanded like a King. Certainly, he was the King in his home.

Aiden and Charlotte's house looked colorful and vibrant beyond the norms of the American picket-fenced suburban living. The front of the house was painted off-white with magenta trims, and the roof, a shade of raw sienna to reflect Aiden and Charlotte's love for exotic locales. Five assorted vehicles parked in the garage, the driveway, and along the curb. A ubiquitous presence of vehicles in the estate depicted the owners' readiness for excursions, road trips, getaways, explorations, and adventures.

Interior-wise, Aiden and Charlotte's abode was not grandiose as what's conjured from a picture-perfect storybook. Rather, it was full of cozy colorful walls decorated with paintings, pictures, knick-knacks, and memorabilia from travels -- corral, lime green, sky blue, lava gray, and shades of Tuscany hues.

Aiden's office, music room and car garage presented a combination of minimalistic décor with a plethora of machinery, tools, instruments, and gadgets. His office was sufficiently equipped with one desktop, two monitors, three laptops, two printers, one paper shredder, and his bookshelf contained the kind of items he preferred to or had time to read: books by James Patterson, Stephen King, Agatha Christie, and The Lord of the Rings, The Hobbit, Star Wars, Star Trek, as well as various fantasy series, mysteries, and epic stories. He had long departed from pursuits of his previous marred life, those dreamy and valiant adventures with Percy Jackson, with all the Marvel or DC heroes to share with his young kids. Those devoted and happy journeys with his kids into the realms of Disney animation were stored in his memory. He retained all the moral lessons learned from Aladdin, Pocahontas, Ariel, Simba, Pinocchio, and Tarzan, but traded the silky and ornate curtains in his home theater with cordless faux wood blinds.

Aiden placed his mother's picture centered and forefront on the mantel. He used his two children's pictures as his wall decorations. The photos of him and Charlotte together were mostly added by Charlotte as an afterthought. Aiden seemed to oftentimes forget that Charlotte was part of his family. As his wife (though the second one at that), she should have been, if not the most important person, but the significant one in his life.

In his music room, Aiden built shelves that held assorted accessories of musical instruments, leaving twenty plus guitars lying around the floor in their hard-shell cases. Above his work bench were industrial shelving units that contained all sorts of gizmos and gadgets, including necessities like toolboxes, tool kits, power drills, electric saws, knives, pliers, wrenches, rulers, levels, headlamps, flashlights, testers, gauges, a pressure washer, a carpet cleaner, three vacuums, five floor jacks, three cable boosters, and many more. To the right of the units, he hung a special organizer with about fifty little drawers that stored nails and screws of various sizes.

On the ceiling of the patio leading to the backyard, Aiden hung ceramic wind chimes, fastened outdoor Christmas lights along the roof eaves, and installed a massive grill underneath the chimes and the lights, where he produced many delicious summer dinners and feasts for guests at gatherings.

Aiden loved to toil in those rooms; they provided a space for him to have his "me time" as well as to labor and sweat off whatever was troubling him. He often sought the relaxation he needed by working in his house and thought over what needed to be pondered and decided in life.

Charlotte's living quarters, her study, kitchen, and recreation room illustrated vividly, her passion for life. Life was a palette with nuanced tinges for her. She loved all sorts of objects: they contained unnamable artistic essences and prompted limitless new learnings. Five bookcases and assorted shelving designs were placed strategically and esthetically to hold her many books and sundry curios. Other than her office desk with several computers, printers, and musical recording devices that served specific purposes, the content of her shelves revealed an evident obsession for "uselessness" of arts.

Charlotte showed abundant love and curiosity for life. There was a thick colorful rug she brought home from Morocco on the floor. On her windowsills were countless miniatures of creatures and objects she acquired: three green tree frogs with human expressions on their faces, two little cute pigs embracing each other, two African elephants with their trunks gesticulating desires of freedom, seven Egyptian camels lining up to form a caravan ready for explorations, three sailboats in different sizes and designs, numerous beautiful precious stones and seashells, eight South American toucans promenading dandily and happily, ten Mexican turtles wearing straw hats loitering about, three Chinese dragons in flying modes, five chess sets with exquisite pieces of sculptured figurines, one Canadian bison carved out of hardwood, miscellaneous glass figurines and ornaments, and a collection of varied wild animals seemingly sauntering in an enclosed sanctuary.

On her refrigerator along with five magnet boards on the wall, Charlotte placed numerous magnets that captured unique sceneries of different countries she traveled to worldwide: Cambodia, Thailand, Vietnam, Taiwan, China, Hong Kong, Macau, Japan, Indonesia, Malaysia, Abu Dhabi, France, Czechoslovakia, Holland, Italy, England, Canada, Mexico, Brazil, Spain, Hungary, Belize, the Caribbean countries, and many others.

As an avid reader, numerous writers had shaped and molded Charlotte's identity. Her book collection was a testimony to her cerebral quest: cultural critical entries of Edward Said, Julia Kriesteva, Jacques Derrida, Michel Faucault, Sigmund Freud, Simone De

Bouvoir, Gayatri Chakravorty Spivak, and writings of great authors such as John Irving, Susan Sontag, Shakespeare, Ray Bradbury, Alice Munro, Italo Calvin, etc. Those spaces with endless articles of beauty and splendor were made to provide not only a safe haven for Charlotte, but to incite creativity, productivity, inspiration, fun, and enjoyment.

While Charlotte was intellectual and introverted, Aiden's appeal or proclivity to popularity was personified in his own brand of humor. His genteel wits principally involved a big heart for everybody. He needed social interactions with his circles of associates. He helped them feel better about their own lives. He shared with them what he and Charlotte planed for the day, for the week, the month, and the year. By connecting with people, he was to make the entire world better, grander, and happier.

Aiden was a firm believer of his own mottos:

"I give compliments to make people feel good and strong."

"I talk therefore I connect the world."

"I assist the needy and so there's less misery in my community."

Aiden paid attention to every detail to make other people's lives easier. He was an altruist at heart.

"I got to rebuild this muscle car to its perfect condition before I can even sell it."

"More cars and carburetors today?" Charlotte wanted to be interested in what he's doing.

She could barely pronounce "carburetors" with confidence, let alone understanding how they worked.

"Yes and no, I ordered a new set of wheel bearings that are supposed to arrive."

"Ok, you're checking the air and fuel for the internal combustion engine, and the air–fuel ratio has to be proper, right? How about those wheels? What's wrong with them now?"

"I have to make sure they are balanced and there's no vibrations."

"How do they work?"

"Honey, if I have to explain everything every single time, I will not finish any work. Just come help me bleed the brake, please."

"Bleed?" Wide eyed, Charlotte wondered why automobile terminology had to be so chauvinistic as Aiden's pals would say: "She rides like a virgin, absolutely sweet and gorgeous" and "she's hot, smooth, and wild."

"Yes, you just press the brake slowly and steadily all the way down and let it go gently -- when I tell you to."

"Down, up, down, up…."

"Yes, perfect."

Perfect was when everyone looked at Aiden's work and showed admiration. Perfect was when everyone sought Aiden's advice for everything and about all things. Perfect was when Aiden was the center of everyone's attention. Perfect was when Aiden commanded the course of his and Charlotte's life together.

When Aiden's world lacked perfection, he yelled and got into furious fits. He often felt obliged to rectify people's problems:

Aiden yelled at the TV set when incompetent or corrupt politicians made their speeches or commented on what anyone was to do with anything. Aiden yelled at the commercials and claimed how stupid American drugs were with all the side effects more harmful than their alleged functions as remedies. Aiden yelled most often at Charlotte, for every little thing that she said or did that for some reason rubbed him the wrong way.

"Don't touch me. I don't feel good."

"Don't even try… It's too hot to cuddle!"

"Don't you try to tell me what to do!"

"Don't make so much food for a whole army!"

"Don't bug me. I have to concentrate on the white paper."

"Don't ask me that question."

"Don't talk like that."

"Don't, don't, don't, don't, don't…."

Charlotte was a worrier and asked on many occasions: "Did you lock your car door?" And Aiden would roar: "What? You think I am an idiot? I can't remember to secure my vehicle?"

Charlotte continued to ask and remind him to heed details in daily life. She continued to pick up empty bottles, pieces of candy wrappers, used paper towels, dirty laundry and dirty dishes on the kitchen counter, his desk, his bedside table, his chair, his car seat, his workbench, the dining table, and the floor. She continued to turn off the lights at night, to watch for a door left unlocked, an unflushed toilet, a continual spinning of the dryer after Aiden removed the clothes from it.

Aiden was the King, and Charlotte held on to that ideal of a husband whose love was so immense that when he loved the whole world and the world around them, he would love her and cherish her the most.

When Aiden said: "My wife loves me very much" -- Charlotte knew that his love for her was equal.

Or, was it? Are men too self-centered to truly love someone else? Are their thinking patterns too liner to involve parallel or peripheral visions that discern emotions or sensitivities concerning other human beings around them? Are they too sensible but too insensitive to detect all that is particularized or experienced in a female's heart?

Charlotte's abundant feelings and sentiments did not propel Aiden to look closer into her inner life. Her longings for independence of mind did not grant her autonomy especially when it involved decisions about what technological or mechanical apparatuses -- things in the realms that Aiden considered to be his territories. He was in a fit of the sulks when she bought a desktop computer, two theatrical binoculars, and three sound recording devices -- without consulting with him first.

One time, Aiden, Charlotte, Vera, and George went to an Escape Room with a bunch of other relatives and friends. Vera, particularly, loved an action-packed adventure to test people's brains and wits, and she pretty much dictated where to go and what to do.

"Hmmm, Steampunk Ship, Cannibal's Feast, Medieval Delight, Mind of A Genius.... I say we go with the Genius room; it sounds more intelligent." Vera proclaimed with a surefire tone in her voice.

"Ok, I second that." George would follow Vera to the edge of a cliff if asked to.

"If we want to do something extraordinary, it's got to be scary. Maybe the cannibals are more fun." Aiden's cousin, Sue Mary Besseler, always liked to be contrary.

"Auntie Sue Mary, you don't want to be eaten. It's more engaging to exercise our minds." Vera insisted on the kitschy cerebral rather than the gory carnal. She would not budge.

Everyone followed Vera into the room and was immediately surrounded by the ambience of a foggy, dark confined space. They first encountered a huge ornate chest with a heavy metal lock on it.

"I do not like to lose, guys. Let's start searching for the key to the lock. Everybody, go!" Vera demanded.

Aiden instantly came to Vera's assistance and said: "Yes, move. Don't stand around. Search!"

George groped around the chest and discovered something bulging underneath the rug on which the chest stood. He gingerly removed a mysterious device from under the weighty wool fabric, which was woven so thickly that a shield seemed to be created to prevent this device from exploding or dissolving before anyone could take a crack at it and found some clue useful for the next step.

"Good job, George!" Vera exclaimed. Excited to lead the first move, she grabbed the piece of paper containing the first clue from George and read: "I do not see with the eyes I may have. Instead, many eyes lay on me and see me as I stare them back."

Everyone shouted out possible answers.

"A camera!" Uncle Jeff was quick to come up with an answer.

"A pair of glasses!" Aiden offered.

"A blindfold!" Auntie Anna added.

"Yes, they are all good. Let's see what we can find here in this room. Any cameras, glasses, or blindfolds in sight?" Aiden analyzed.

"Maybe there are something hidden behind those 'photos.' The answer might be photos!" Charlotte deducted.

Vera was fast to race to all the photos hanging on the wall and lifted them all up to find a key tapped at the back of one of the picture frames.

"Here we are. A key to the chest!" Vera shouted triumphantly and opened the chest to retrieve a scroll of augury.

On the scroll was a drawing of some sort, faded and torn from a suggested passage of time. Everyone gathered around the drawing and tried to determine what the image was about. It looked to be an animal or creature of some mystic origin.

After many failed attempts at different directions in the room, Aiden detected a dragon-like physique and proposed a hunt for dragon bones.

Presently everyone was stumping and groping around to see if any concealed devices would hold relevant hints. Uncle Jeff started staring at all the images on the wall, trying to decode hidden messages from them. One sketch of a 19th century aristocrat especially caught his attention.

"Look at the lines and strokes! There are words written along them." He called out to everyone.

All eyes were on the text:

"'Einstein's Riddle: Who Has the Fish? – is written there!" Aiden shouted excitedly.

Everyone was conjuring up their memories about that riddle. Although they could not name the details, they were able to solve that clue by guessing and exploring each location of the objects in the room. Later that day, they would look up the riddle and analyze it:

> There are five houses in five different colors.

In each house lives a person with a different nationality.
These five owners drink a certain type of beverage, smoke a certain brand of cigar and keep a certain pet.
No owners have the same pet, smoke the same brand of cigar or drink the same beverage.
The question is: Who owns the fish?
These are your hints:
The Brit lives in the red house;
The Swede keeps dogs as pets;
The Dane drinks tea;
The green house is on the left of the white house;
The green house's owner drinks coffee;
The person who smokes Pall Mall rears birds;
The owner of the yellow house smokes Dunhill;
The man living in the center house drinks milk;
The Norwegian lives in the first house;
The man who smokes blends lives next to the one who keeps cats;

> The man who keeps horses lives next to the man who smokes Dunhill;
> The owner who smokes BlueMaster drinks beer;
> The German smokes Prince;
> The Norwegian lives next to the blue house;
> The man who smokes blend has a neighbor who drinks water."

They came up with the analysis together. Starting with the fives; they were able to find the answer: The German has the fish.

- The five nationalities are:
  - Norwegian
  - Brit
  - Swede
  - Dane
  - German
- The five colors are:
  - Red
  - Green
  - White
  - Yellow
  - Blue
- The five beverages are:

    - Tea
    - Coffee
    - Milk
    - Beer
    - Water
- The five cigars are:
    - Pall Mall
    - Dunhill
    - Blends
    - BlueMaster
    - Prince
- The five pets are:
    - Dogs
    - Birds
    - Cats
    - Horses
    - Fish

They drew matrixes and deducted in the following tables.

The five houses are in a row, numbered from left to right. The Norwegian is in the first house:

House	*#1*	*#2*	*#3*	*#4*	*#5*

Color	?	?	?	?	?
Natl	Norweg	?	?	?	?
Bevg	?	?	?	?	?
Smokes	?	?	?	?	?
Pet	?	?	?	?	?

Since the Brit lives in the red house, the Norwegian can't. The Norwegian lives next to the blue house, so his house isn't blue. The green house is to the left of the white house; the Norwegian can't live in the white house since there is no house to the left, and can't live in the green house because his only neighbor, the one to the right, is known to live in the blue house. Therefore, the Norwegian lives in the yellow house.

The owner of the yellow house smokes Dunhill, and the Norwegian has a neighbor with a blue house (the Norwegian only has one neighbor, to the right.)

House	#1	#2	#3	#4	#5

Color	Yellow	Blue	?	?	?
Natl	Norweg	?	?	?	?
Bevg	?	?	?	?	?
Smokes	Dunhill	?	?	?	?
Pet	?	?	?	?	?

The man who keeps horses lives next to the man who smokes Dunhill, and so the horse owner lives in the blue house. The center house's owner drinks milk, the green house's owner drinks coffee, and the green house is to the left of the white house. Since the left two houses are the yellow and blue houses, the only position for the green and white are green as the fourth and white as the fifth. The middle (third) drinks milk and the owner of the green house drinks coffee. The middle house should be red, and therefore is the Brit's.

House	*#1*	*#2*	*#3*	*#4*	*#5*
Color	Yellow	Blue	Red	Green	White

Natl	Norweg	?	Brit	?	?
Bevg	?	?	Milk	Coffee	?
Smokes	Dunhill	?	?	?	?
Pet	?	Horse	?	?	?

The owner who smokes BlueMaster drinks beer. Since neither houses #3 and #4 drink beer and house #1 does not smoke BlueMaster, the only possibilities are houses #2 and #5. With that in mind, it is evident house #1 cannot drink beer (only house #2 or #5 can). The only possible beverages for house #1 are water and tea, but since the Dane drinks tea, house #1 drinks water. The man who smokes Blends lives next to someone who drinks water; the only house next to #1 (the water-drinking house) is #2. The man who smokes Blends lives next to the one who has cats; so the cat-house is #1 or #3.

House	*#1*	*#2*	*#3*	*#4*	*#5*
Color	Yellow	Blue	Red	Green	White

Natl	Norweg	?	Brit	?	?
Bevg	Water	B/T?	Milk	Coffee	B/T?
Smokes	Dunhill	Blends	?	?	?
Pet	Cat?	Horse	Cat?	?	?

Since the Dane drinks tea, he must live in either house #2 or #5. The Swede and German could live in house #2, #4 or #5.

House	*#1*	*#2*	*#3*	*#4*	*#5*
Color	Yellow	Blue	Red	Green	White
Natl	Norweg	D/S/G?	Brit	S/G?	D/S/G?
Bevg	Water	B/T?	Milk	Coffee	B/T?
Smokes	Dunhill	Blends	?	?	?
Pet	Cat?	Horse	Cat?	?	?

The beer-drinker smokes BlueMaster. The only houses that could drink beer are #2 and #5. But #2 smokes Blends, #5 must be the house which drinks beer and smokes BlueMaster, and #2 must be the house that drinks tea and the house of the Dane. It is possible that the Dane's residence being house #5.

House	*#1*	*#2*	*#3*	*#4*	*#5*
Color	Yellow	Blue	Red	Green	White
Natl	Norweg	Dane	Brit	S/G?	S/G?
Bevg	Water	Tea	Milk	Coffee	Beer
Smokes	Dunhill	Blends	?	?	BlueM
Pet	Cat?	Horse	Cat?	?	?

The German smokes Prince. Therefore, he could not live at house #5 and therefore must live at house #4. The Swede must live at house #5; house #5 raises dogs since the Swede raises dogs, and that house #4 smokes Prince since the German smokes Prince.

House	*#1*	*#2*	*#3*	*#4*	*#5*
Color	Yellow	Blue	Red	Green	White

Natl	Norweg	Dane	Brit	German	Swede
Bevg	Water	Tea	Milk	Coffee	Beer
Smokes	Dunhill	Blends	?	Prince	BlueM
Pet	Cat?	Horse	Cat?	?	Dogs

The only possibility for house #3's smokes is Pall Mall; all of the others are taken. Whoever smokes Pall Mall raises birds; so house #3 raises birds, and house #1 therefore has cats, since the only houses which could have had cats were #1 and #3, and #3 has been eliminated.

House	*#1*	*#2*	*#3*	*#4*	*#5*
Color	Yellow	Blue	Red	Green	White
Natl	Norweg	Dane	Brit	German	Swede
Bevg	Water	Tea	Milk	Coffee	Beer
Smokes	Dunhill	Blends	PallM	Prince	BlueM
Pet	Cat	Horse	Birds	?	Dogs

The only remaining pet is the fish, which must be owned by the German.

House	*#1*	*#2*	*#3*	*#4*	*#5*
Color	Yellow	Blue	Red	Green	White
Natl	Norweg	Dane	Brit	German	Swede
Bevg	Water	Tea	Milk	Coffee	Beer
Smokes	Dunhill	Blends	PallM	Prince	BlueM
Pet	Cat	Horse	Birds	Fish	Dogs

Presently, Vera stumbled upon the part of the wall that was marked "Entry to Germany" and opened a secret passageway. Aiden pushed through everyone to stand aside his daughter. He needed to be the trophy holder, along with Vera, in that triumphant moment. He and Vera both holding the found treasure, raised their arms to show the key case high up in the air and claim victory: "Here we are -- the key to the escape door! Woohoo!"

The moment of glory was shared by the King and the Princess -- as usual, everyone else was just there to witness their magnificent feat. No one could fight them to take away their credit. They had to have their acclamation of victory all to themselves. Aiden would subsequent recite again and again, how wonderful and brilliant his daughter was, even years after the family adventure.

Aiden performed a king's duties; he kept peace, rescued people, protected everyone, and supported all, especially his Princess Vera and Prince George. Aiden was the King, the center of the universe, and his children, the nucleus of his adoration and obsession.

7. I Am the Good Child

My name is Vera Melone Davis. I lived with Dad till I was 12, and then I had to go back north to live with Mom and George. I missed Dad a lot, but it was good to be with Mom and my brother again -- if only Dad could be with us, too. He said that he traveled too much and heard that Mom had cleaned up quite a bit, and so it was OK for me to go back to live with her. Mom had stayed away from drugs and alcohol for six months straight, and so I was moving in with her, instead of having a hired nanny watching over me all the time when Dad had to travel for business.

I liked to think my homecoming as a mission to take care of George and Mom. It's true that I am always the mature one; I am the good child. George is too reckless and undisciplined. Mom needed me, and my brother – he just couldn't be left alone by himself with Mom; he would raise havoc and hindered Mom's path to sobriety. He would not survive another distressful episode with a recovering addict for a mom who couldn't even look out for herself. He was only 8.

I remember the joy of reuniting with Mom and George. They came out to meet me at the train stop. Mom brought a new dress she shopped for months for me and had me change right at the restroom of the train station.

"Living with your father makes you a tomboy, which is ok. But I want you to show you're a young woman, too. Now, put this on." Mom said indignantly.

"I got this flower for you." George handed me a red rose.

I was so happy to see them and so touched that I cried for hours straight.

I helped George with his schoolwork and played with him every evening. Watching him grow made me feel like an adult. I would deduce the logic behind his daily learnings or troubles, and teach him valuable academic and life lessons.

"You'll get another detention if you don't keep your eyes on the teacher and the board as instructed." I told George after he got in-house suspension for doodling on his desk, not keeping his eyes on the board or the teacher.

"Why? I was learning all the same without looking at Ms. Kim!"

"I understand, but you have to show courtesy. A classroom is a social setting where you gain knowledge, and learn how to get along with people, too."

Sometimes, George's inattentiveness could be annoying. I know better being a big sister of a wayward child whose mind is set on musical beats more than the norms or manners a school daily routine requires.

I am always savvy about academics and popular at school and all. George, on the other hand, does not care at all about schoolwork. He would finish homework assignments as soon as he could and dragged me to take a stroll, run down the street, or play hide-and-seek with him.

I watched how small he was but how big his dreams were: he wanted to transcend the limitations of the mundane world and soar in the larger realms of his imagination and aspiration, like songs, tunes, sports, games, pranks, mischiefs, and shenanigans.

George grew to be a handful kind of boy. He would make such messes in the house, or fall from all sorts of trees, slides, and walls. When he was 8, he made smaller, manageable messes. When he grew to be a teen, the messes got bigger and uncontrollable.

"I want Skittles and nuggets for dinner." Little George flopped down on his seat at the dining table, still sneaking glances at his video games on the big TV screen, but readily demanding what he felt like at that moment.

"You need to eat this plate of Broccoli before eating anything sweet." I insisted like a know-how older sister.

"No, I don't."

"Yes, you do."

"No, I don't. What're you gonna do with it?"

"Nothing. I will do nothing and give you nothing to eat if you don't eat like a normal person."

"Ok, then. I will keep playing games." George hopped back to sit in front of the TV set, unyielding and adamant.

By the time I finished dinner with Mom and came to check George in the living room, he had managed to decorate the entire floor with colorful pieces of candies, his face smeared with juices of rainbow-like hues.

"What's going on here?" I asked patiently.

"Just trying to have some dinner!"

"You do not have candies for dinner. You are only allowed sweets or disserts after regular meals." I told it like what should have been.

"Don't tell me what to do. I can do whatever I want."

"Clean up your own mess." I insisted.

"No. You clean up." He pouted.

I gave George sisterly stern looks and walked away. But I didn't seem to be able to walk away from all his troubles and problems later in his life.

After I returned to live with Mom and George, I was always the one George sought out when he needed solutions. I was always the one he consulted with when Dad, living in a different city, had not an inkling of all the secretive details about his wild, wanton, and uninhibited life.

George grew to be a teen-star and had so many buddies and fans one could not begin to count. He started DJing when he was 13. And the messes he made grew with his expanded circles of hommies.

"Yo, wassup? Let's hang out in my basement studio tonight. Let's jam!"

As a teen, George was precocious and befriended people from high schools, colleges, bars, and other performance venues. George and his friends would smoke and play loud music into the wee hours in Mom's basement, his studio pro tempore until he gets famous and rich enough to buy a big mansion himself.

Once George burned the carpet in the basement because he and his friends all fell into a trance after too many drinks. Some girl even got scorched by the fire; her hair caught on fire and formed a perm with peculiar mixed smells only cigarettes, acholic beverages, and bonfires could produce -- big messes! He partied on and ignored me and Mom.

I had to give George ultimatums: if he refused to discipline himself, Mom and I would have to send him away. Where to? I had no plan, but something's got to give. He caused Mom and me too many grievances and headaches. He claimed he liked "trolling" and was a master of clever tricks and jokes.

Eventually Dad suggested to send George to the East Coast to live with him and his new wife, Charlotte. George was 15 and going on 30 or 3. No amount of harness would keep that wild animal in line. Only Dad could do it -- hopefully.

Now I miss George and Dad tremendously. And I have reestablished a strong connection and bond with my brother, George. To me, George is always my little brother. He may be a big star and music producer one day. I hope he is. I am very proud of how he has grown to be more of a respectable young man. Well, he still now and then, pulls business of devilment, of rascality. But he is, more or less, self-governing, and self-determining -- after Dad and Charlotte urged him to move out of their house at the age of 18.

That Bad Old Little George!

Enough about George. I am Vera, the good child, the mature and capable one. I shouldn't have to feel that Dad is partial to George now that they're living in the same city and doing things together all the time. How come Dad is not here to fix every car problem I have? George will still have his cell phone on a "family plan" at the age of 50! George will get double doses of Christmas every year. George gets to have Dad help him with all sorts of issues in his life. George is damned lucky!

I should be the one Dad looks after every day. I am his Princess! I call the shots. I am the smart one -- the good child to boot. I manage to finish college without Dad alongside me telling me how important education is. I manage to obtain a good-paying job with the local government. I manage to take care of Mom's belongings and distribute her assets after she passed away. Ah, how sad and tragic that day was when Mom fell on the floor, white foams forming around the corners of her mouth ….

"Mom, Mom ….what's … wrong?!" I stammered out of breath, in shock seeing her lying there unable to move.

No answer.

"Mom …. Mom! Please wake up!" No matter how I bagged, she would not respond.

"911 -- I need an ambulance quick!"

Mom passed away in the hospital without anyone else present but me and George. George was in a state of catatonic stupor for weeks. I alone, had to act and take care of everything.

In fact, I always take care of things for everyone around me. I take care of Dad's sadness by cheering him up with my incessant talks and laughs, I take care of Mom's dependence on substances by cleaning up after her and urging her to sobriety during her frequent relapses, and I take care of George's messes by instilling moral values -- well, at least I try anyhow. I even take care of the repairs around my house because my husband Brandon has no clues how to. I am the one wearing pants in the household. I dominate every detail in my life with Brandon: where to go, what to eat, what company to keep, how to dress, how to make ends meet, and how to act ....

I pretty much determine that Charlotte cannot be in my life; I block her out. So, Brandon and George must follow suits. Yes, I only visit Dad, not Charlotte. Whatever is going on in my life, or Brandon's or George's life, is none of charlotte's business. She has no say whatsoever as to what is going on or how we go about our lives.

"If you want to come visit, Vera, my wife has to be treated better!" Dad once told me I had to play nice. I was so pissed I could cancel the whole trip to visit Dad!

"Why! I AM nice. Who says I ain't nice?" I insisted for Dad to see my merits and how Charlotte should not be part of anything.

"Please, Honey ...." Dad sounded so sad on the phone that I finally said: "OK. Your daughter comes to see you only once a year, can't you spend all your time with me, please?"

"Sure, we'll do all kinds of fun things. But Charlotte needs to be included in some of the things, OK?" Dad implored.

"OK!"

I can't believe I have to be forced to spend time with Charlotte. How repulsive! A woman who steals Dad from us! But no matter, I know I am the Princess. I know no one can take the center stage even if they try. I will have my dad to myself as I wish. I will not allow anyone to take away any precious together-time of Dad and me.

8. Charlotte's Business

A man who loves his parents more than his wife will end up being divorced; a man who loves his children more than his wife will always be single. The reason is that a happy wife takes care of the elderly and the young, and a neglected wife causes everyone in a family to become miserable like her. Happy wife, happy life, as one may conclude.

Aiden's parents had long passed. His immense love was given to others with such vigor that it often denoted a resolve for redemption, as if by loving other people he had been able to reclaim some time with his parents. He took care of people and was extra attentive to his children. His love had no limit when it concerned his kids.

It was a habit of Aiden's to want to know all details in his children's lives. Others including Charlotte, were like garnishes and condiments to the main dishes and centerpieces. Charlotte often felt like an outsider when Aiden engaged in his daily conversations with Vera and George.

Not Charlotte's business -- Aiden was content to comply with Vera's decree. What could go wrong so long as he accommodated his children's wishes? Heaven knows that it was Charlotte's business when Vera and George wanted to come visit -- Charlotte was the one who had to put them up and cook them meals. It was Charlotte's business when those children had their birthdays or whatever occasions to celebrate.

It was Charlotte's business when Aiden and Charlotte drew up their living will. Vera and George had to have a portion of Charlotte's assets. It was Charlotte's business when many a time her travel plans had to be changed and rearranged around Aiden's children's schedules. Of course, it was Charlotte's business; it involved Charlotte. Her life was inevitably entangled with Aiden's children's.

Charlotte wanted out! She tried staying away when Aiden took care of his children's problems. She avoided George every time he came running for his dad's rescue or attention. She kept at a distance so that no excessive tangled emotions could further thwart her feelings of a happy life with Aiden.

One time Charlotte's convinced Aiden to check out the new shopping complex in town with her. They went more for window shopping than acquiring extra items they didn't really need.

"Let go check out the new shops." Charlotte was enthused about new findings.

"OK, George's birthday is coming up. We will go." His son birthday was the first thing that associated with shopping for Aiden.

"I am not shopping. I just wanted to check out the new place," muttered Charlotte with incredulity. Here again they were talking about shopping for George.

"Do whatever you want; I will pick up something for my son." Aiden ignored anything Charlotte had in mind and went on his merry way to fulfill his duty as a loving father.

Aiden went straight to buy birthday presents for George, while Charlotte bought clothes for herself and her husband. Almost every excursion or trip Aiden and Charlotte took by themselves was never completely their own time together. Aiden's children constant phone-calls and needs or demands often threw them off. Marrying to a man with kids can mean losing control of one's own life. Charlotte's stigma was that her sense of imbalance not only derived from

Aiden's kids' rejection, but her own resistance to crossing oceans when the kids could not come to terms with change in their family.

Another time George stayed in the city for Christmas instead of going up north to his sister and his grandparents as usual. Charlotte bought presents and cooked up a storm only to have George complain about little everything.

"I am a creator and so I am a vegan – cleansing inside and out." George was very proud of his own beliefs and philosophies concerning veganism, albeit an avid pot smoker.

"OK. I have the meatloaf made of lentils. You can have it with assorted vegetables on the side." Charlotte offered.

"Hmnn -- it smells weird, but what else is there to eat?" George was his same pompous and ungrateful self.

The next day, he moaned and criticized: "Do I have to eat leftovers?"

And the next day he continued: "There's nothing I can eat in this house!"

"Have some cereals or dry foods for breakfast -- there are a lot of snacks in the cabinet." Charlotte suggested with a good intention.

"Why don't you go eat poop? Don't tell me what to eat." Out of nowhere, George came back with a malicious reply to Charlotte, perhaps mistaking her offer as an attempt to control or command him.

Charlotte was lambasted for no reason, and she exploded with hurt feelings: "What kind of thing is that to say to anyone? Who do you think you are?!"

George's visit was more a drag than family bliss, like many times before. Charlotte tried to maintain her daily routine, while George drank up 48 bottles of beers every day. So much for his "cleansing inside and out"!

Aiden went between Charlotte and George trying to smooth things over. With attentive solicitude, he proposed an activity to cheer everyone up: "Let's go see a show or a movie …." But the awkwardness between Charlotte and Aiden's kids was indelible.

Vera came visit once with her friend Lisa. The girls were out and about sightseeing every day. They came back to Aiden and Charlotte's house with meals ready-made on the dining table.

"I don't eat ribs!" Vera eyed the table full of dishes and cried out right away.

"You can try. Honey, it's delicious." Aiden urged her.

"Why? I will not have ribs." Vera rolled her eyes and insisted.

"I will have a bite." Vera's friend Lisa tried to ease the tension in the air: "Hmmm.... It's really yummy."

"Let's enjoy the meal. No more nitpicking." Aiden's urged again.

Charlotte made it her business to make sure that the guests felt welcome. She even bought presents for the girls to take home. At the end of their visit, they presented a thank-you gift to Aiden.

"Thank you, Dad, for your hospitality. Here is something for you to remember us by." Vera gave Aiden the thank- you note and completely disregarded Charlotte as if Charlotte hadn't lived in the house.

Lisa happily packed Charlotte's present for her, while Vera left hers untouched on the living-room couch!

It was like that with Vera and George. Charlotte was treated worse than a stranger. Charlotte made it her business to let her grievances known to Aiden. She kept at a distance from his children because of their rudeness and meanness toward her. When Aiden failed to sympathize with her feelings of resentment, she took actions.

"Where are you? Are you going to answer your phone?"

Aiden's voice mails revealed his agitation.

"Where are you?"

"Where are you?"

"Where the heck are you?!"

"Where are you? Please answer your phone."

"Are you safe? Please call home."

"Are you lost? Lost your phone?"

. . . .

Charlotte checked into a hotel in the next town over. Her silent objection did not help the matter. Aiden's reaction was as usual, further distanced her and boxed her in a frantic frame of mind, feeling misunderstood and uncherished.

Aiden was not the greatest at dealing with confrontations. He typically got so furious that he withdrew from any formats of communication. His reaction was to assume that Charlotte left him for good or was mugged somewhere. He did not make efforts to look for her or investigate where she could be. Instead, he transferred all the money in their joint account into George's account, thinking Charlotte or her mugger would get hold of the savings!

Charlotte was dumbfounded returning to a grumpy husband.

"Why is the money all gone?" Charlotte asked.

"How would I know what happened to you? You could have been kidnapped and all your possessions taken!" Aiden uttered his protest with rage.

"You didn't even think about looking me up at my favorite getaways?" She was not happy about her husband's lack of intent to make things right.

"You're unbelievable. What do you expect me to do? I am transferring the money right back now that you're back." Aiden was short-fused; his love could spread far and wide to everyone, but the very person he needed to show affection for did not get enough tenderness or devotion.

Charlotte would not submit to unfair treatment or neglect. She demanded to be seen. If only her resentment could open Aiden's eyes. He turned a blind eye to his and his children's self-centeredness. Charlotte had to get away, at least for a while ....

9. He Was Just Resting His Eyes

"I am not sleeping; I am just resting my eyes." Aiden would often say to Charlotte, his eyes closed when they were doing things together, watching TV or a movie, reading, or playing games.

He got his very much needed rest by intermittently closing his eyes during their pastime activities. Another way to help him relax was to go online and browse through mindless social media posts and messages. His "quiet wakefulness" allowed him to reset. In the process he often could not hear what Charlotte was saying to him.

"Are you sleeping now? Should I change to a different show?" Charlotte didn't want him to miss any part of the show they were watching.

"…." No answer.

"Are you watching?"

"…." No answer.

"Should I pause the show and get some snacks?"

"…." No answer.

"OK. I am going to pause the show now."

"I am just resting my eyes." Finally, Aiden responded and implied that he was still "listening to" the show.

Aiden was hard of hearing seemingly only around his wife. He was responsive to every word his children utter. For every ounce of thoughtfulness he showed for Charlotte, it seemed quintupled for others, especially for George and Vera. Perhaps he felt guilty about baring his love for Charlotte so inadvertently that he would hurt his children's feelings. He would immediately follow up with a call or a message to report every detail to his children after a particular good time spent with Charlotte.

"Hey, how are you doing. We're just taking our motorhome for a drive. How about you? Are you planning to do anything fun this weekend?" Aiden called up George on the highway, putting him on speaker phone through the sound system.

"I am just chilln' with some buddies. Can I come over to borrow a guitar for my performance tonight?" George always needed something from his father -- a good-looking and better-sounding guitar than the one he bought himself, a guitar case for his road trip, a tool for fixing his often-broken-down car, his health insurance card replacement, some cookies his father made, a cool hat his father wore that he loved so much .... The list of things he wanted from his father never seemed to end.

"Sure, come over. We will be home round 4:00 PM." Many of Aiden and Charlotte's trips had to be cut short because George wanted something from Dad.

"When do you have time to gab? We are at a dance, believe it or not. And I am dancing!" Aiden called up Vera to describe where he and Charlotte were, what they were doing, and who they were hanging out with.

"Wow, isn't that cool. You old folks can still have fun!" Vera approved.

"Yeah, we even have a poker tournament planned tomorrow."

"Fantastic! Report back and let me know if you win any money." Vera commanded and Aiden obeyed.

"Guess who won the tournament?"

"Not you?"

"Yes, me! The smart and handsome one. I even won the whole pot with nata in one game. You have no idea how fun it is to win after so many rounds …."

Aiden not only described all the good times to his children, but also said things to boost their egos. He was also inclined to yell at Charlotte in front of them.

"George is working for the big stars and getting access to the inside circles now." Sitting together with George and his friends at a restaurant, Aiden proudly said to Charlotte.

"Hmm…." Charlotte said nothing to flame his showiness. To her, "working for a big star" did not impress or amount to signify of one's success.

"What? You say nothing to that? Nothing impresses you!?" Aiden raised his voice at the table just to display to his son how he supported him and stood up for him.

"You don't need to yell at me." Charlotte protested.

"I am not yelling at you. Just trying to get you to see how great George is doing."

"OK. All good." Charlotte suppressed her discontentment.

"Yes, George is doing great! I was not nearly as successful as he is now at the age of 25."

It gave Aiden the greatest satisfaction while ostentatiously touting and flaunting his children's accomplishment and brilliance. Their achievement was Aiden's favorite subject of conversations on any occasions. He could turn any topics of discussion into something about his own children's insurmountable talents, or about his first or current wife's attributes.

Once at a casual business dinner, a colleague of Aiden's was telling his niece's story: a young mother's difficult life and her missed opportunities in life.

"Nowadays people should not get married too young because you have no idea what you want in life yet at a young age. My niece got married when she was twenty and had two kids by the age of twenty-five. She is now regretting not finishing college. On top of that, she is having a hard time juggling with her two kids and low-paying jobs."

"I will tell you that you just need to have a direction early on; it's not how young you are when you get married. You know who will be the greatest mother? My daughter. She just has the incredible ability to take care of people, and herself. She finished her studies at twenty-five and has had a government job since. She is married at the age of twenty-eight. She doesn't want to have kids yet. But when she does, she will be the most remarkable mother!" Aiden did not respond to his colleague, but instead, narrated Vera's and George's respective lives in chronological orders.

Aiden's love for people was immense. Indeed, he could relate to anyone's life by circling back to reflect on his own, chiefly relating to Vera's and

George's. His way of recounting his or his family's life experiences did not turn people off. Instead, they listened with awe and wonder. They enjoyed his detailing of his own life stories.

To Charlotte, the person who lived with Aiden day in, day out, Aiden's way of associating with the world was endearing, but at times, self-absorbed. She understood that behind the charming stories, there lay a sort of blindness, namely justified egocentrism. She read the hidden lines that depicted Aiden's own brand of patronizing but merited viewpoints.

To others, Aiden was the most funny and engaging person they ever met. He conveyed a sense of camaraderie. He often elicited fellowship that derived from sharing of the human common destiny. He sought the company of the whole world, and in turn, he was the best company one could have!

10. My Resentment Is Consuming Me

I was Charlotte Lewis before marrying Aiden William Melone. I have changed my name to Charlotte Lewis Melone. Ironically, I often feel detached from both the Lewises and the Melones, and at the same time, overly tender toward them. I grew up with strict disciplines and moral values that imparted me with a self-sufficient life path at an early age. Ever since college, graduate schools, and advanced career trainings, I was charting courses on my own dime. I learned earlier on to be frugal, to look at life through perpetual self-reflection and acquisition of knowledge and experience. I never aspire to materialistic gains or achievements, but follow my passions for literature and arts. I am not rich or famous, but I do just fine and well -- I have a fantastic marketing job where I get to utilize my expertise to incorporate arts and sciences to achieve ambitions and goals. I have a wonderful husband who I love dearly and who loves me in return.

However, my relationship with Aiden has been falling short of perfection. I was naïve to think that I could be the best stepmom in the whole world because why not -- I intended to love Vera and George as my own. But no, they reject me. I have learned not to expect anything from them and keep at a distance through all these years of trying, repositioning, being disappointed, being OK with the letdowns, being hurt again and again, and then being stuck in a place where my emotions are bottled up, shot inside, stagnant, and heavy.

I do not agree with Vera's and George's senses of entitlement. Vera's prerogative is to be the apple in Aiden's eye, whereas George thinks everything that belongs to Aiden (and me) should be at his disposal, time, money, resources, properties and all. Vera disregards her father's wife for her own emotional need and safety; George seizes aggressively every opportunity he gets to take anything from his father and stepmother. His grandiose sense of himself is so massive that even Vera feels unbalanced when he gets to have Aiden back him up just about every little detail in his life.

"How come you're selling your west-coast property to George?" Vera called up Aiden and questioned.

"Oh, it's just a thought. Because your brother doesn't have his own house yet and Charlotte and I don't really need a house in the Southwest, we are thinking that may be a good arrangement." Aiden offered his explanation to Vera.

"But how come Brandon and I never got the opportunity to buy your house with your help? Are you giving everything in the house to George?" Vera's voice almost had a trace of anger.

"No no no, we are not giving it to him. We are selling. Anyway, it's just a thought. Don't worry about it." Aiden was comforting Vera.

A thought is enough to trigger George's immediate phone call to his sister to tell her about having access to the house. Vera makes sure she doesn't get the short end of the bargain, while George considers himself the "legitimate and natural" buyer of the house that belongs to my husband and me.

I feel obligated to shed some light on self-sufficiency and independence. But as an "outsider," I only harbor more resentment toward those kids, not being able to speak my mind freely: "You know your parents' properties are not yours!"

Aiden, on the other hand, is always pampering his children and lets their senses of entitlement grow rampant, unbridled and encroaching upon our life together.

"If you want to buy our west-coast house, you can save up some money for down-payment, we will see about helping you to get a loan." Aiden has signed on a car loan for George, covered George in his health insurance plan, put George's cell phone in our family plan, allowed George to use every tool and gadget in our household. His love for George excessive, without any boundaries.

I resent and disapprove the entitlement of Vera and George as well as the leniency exhibited by my own husband, Aiden. Aiden does not understand the Spanish philosopher, Maimonides:

"Give a man a fish and you feed him for a day; teach a man to fish and you feed him for a lifetime." Aiden gives and gives until his children see not limits; his leniency produces bad consequences in his children's and our lives.

I am also aware that it's not healthy to harbor a complex variety of feelings: anger, disappointment, bitterness, and negative emotions. I try to process and analyze my loss of trust. I do not empathize with Aiden because my feelings are unheard and uncared-for. My resentment is consuming me! My thoughtfulness and unconditional support for my husband dwindles over time, and at times, I do not feel close to him at all.

I certainly don't feel close to Vera or George. When they call on the phone, I feel interrupted. When Aiden's brother, sister-in-law, or others call on the phone or come for a visit, I am delighted -- and grateful to be part of a great family. I have tried to let go of my own expectations of my husband and to give him space to do whatever he desires with his children. I stay out of their interactions, but I only become more alienated.

I go back and forth from trying to get close to pulling apart, and from being distant to trying to reconcile again, and again. In the process, I only get hurt, not more at peace or wiser. I guess I have no control over Aiden's children's manners toward me, but I do have the power to see it like what it is and be fine with it.

"I wish all haters die in a global pandemic, especially you know who!" George once openly spoke his mind in front of Aiden and me, insinuating I am "the hater in his life."

"Son, watch what you're saying." Even Aiden could sense George's caustic intent.

"Yep. The world is over-populated anyway. Life has no meaning anyway." George could be dark at times.

While George is haphazardly interacting with me, Vera is averting my existence altogether.

"Your wife is coming too, right? You and your wife will be sitting far from the bride and groom's table." Vera was going over the details of her wedding with Aiden.

"Take Brandon and me out to dinner the night before to make sure you understand what needs to be done." Vera demanded Aiden to do things, typically.

Well, that's what it's like. I should be fine with George wishing me to die. I should let Vera's jealousy and insecurity be. Why imbibe the toxic portion and expect to get better while waiting for others to change? Why not develop my own harmony and allow myself space and time to reach equilibrium? I need to get away. I am leaving my husband for a little while ….

11. The Smell of Books in a Small Town

Charlotte bolted for a small town nearest to the city where she and Aiden lived. She loved the big cities, and she also desired the tranquility of small towns from time to time. She often packed one book she was reading along with her change of clothes for a weekend away from the city. She needed time and space to herself, to just do things, meditate, read, write, create, or think. She felt rested when she had produced something tangible or intangible during her alone time. She enjoyed very much just to read and concentrate on the world a book created for her. The smell of books in a small town made her content, at ease, and even happy.

Driving down the highway, Charlotte turned off her cellphone and listened to the stereo blaring her favorite songs. The music coupled with the wide field of view registered in her as she sped through the scenic drive gave her a sense of freedom, privacy, and satisfaction. It was through this process of letting go, she could come to a halt, position herself in a personal space, all secured and cozy just for her to think things over and find herself again. She would have, have, and have this intimacy with her inner self to practice regaining equilibrium. It would not matter how much and how often she felt denied of her sense of self, she could always come back refreshed, poised, and ready to face the world with calm and patience again.

She knew Aiden would be frantic not hearing back from her, but she needed to crawl into a space where she could take time to seal the hole in her heart, and acquire an impenetrable zone, safe and insulated from all harms, to decompress and to find a direction she needed to move toward in life.

"Sorry, Aiden. I can't reply to your messages right now. Give me some time." Charlotte muttered to the air in her small hotel room as if Aiden had heard her.

"Sorry, Aiden. I need to cry a bit when no one is around." She gestured to the air.

"Am I not visible to you? Aiden? Why are you not seeing or hearing your wife?" She questioned and tried to be assertive about getting her husband to be responsive.

But no, Aiden was furious and would not understand her need for a time-out. He yelled and cursed via the text messages he sent Charlotte. When she came home after two days, he threatened to move out.

"What is going on with you? You couldn't even answer my texts?"

"I just needed time to think."

"There's no excuse for that! Why are you so upset? Because George said something or did something wrong -- because of something I have no control over?! If we cannot all get along, there's no point staying together. I am looking for an apartment to rent now."

"But you could teach your kids how to behave, couldn't you? You could avoid feeding into their big egos!"

"Just go away. I don't want to talk now."

Aiden would shut down when anyone criticized him or his children. Aiden had no problems throwing away his marriage to either protect the visage of his grandeur, or to accommodate his children. Charlotte realized that she could be replaced easily in her own husband's mind, whereas his kids would always be his -- no replacements possible.

That realization propelled Charlotte to limber up and try connecting with Aiden. She was willing to adjust.

"I just don't feel seen or heard any more. I need you to be a bit more considerate, please."

"OK, if we can't stick together, why force it?"

"That's precisely the point. We need to be on the same page." Charlotte tried getting Aiden to understand.

"We are on the same page. Don't I do what you wish and make you happy?" Aiden thought he was the greatest husband, and father or friend.

But Aiden couldn't be the greatest of everything to everyone. He pleased one person and left out another; he took care of everything and ended up short-changing his own life with Charlotte. It was like flying multiple kites at the same time, he lifted one up, dropped the rest, and then switched to let another soar and fail to keep others up in the sky. The kites could not all fly at the same height. There needed to be one focal point of collaboration to successfully coordinate the flying of the kites. Aiden and Charlotte needed to collaborate to keep every kite poised, knowing its coordinates, and hovering on its own accord, without heavy lifting from one single force of wind.

It was also a matter of common courtesy. No one could maintain civilities if there was no fair give-and-take. Pretend civilities would not serve any purpose but hurt chances of open and honest communications.

Charlotte was a trooper for women's rights for nondiscriminatory treatment. Aiden was obtuse about how his desire for popularity might translate into egocentricity to her. She opened up and said frankly to him:

"I hope you consider how I feel when you are busy tending to others and ignore what I have to say."

"I never mean to neglect or hurt you," said Aiden candidly.

"We got to work together and be on the same page," suggested Charlotte.

"Yes, we're always better together."

"Then, don't be short-fused and wanting to move out when things don't go your way."

Aiden and Charlotte stayed together; they were happy in their conjugal life for the most part. Charlotte craved the smells of books in small towns, but she invited Aiden to travel and explore the world instead of hiding in her own sealed space most of the time. Aiden tried to consider and share with his co-pilot, Charlotte. He did not always notice minute details and complex human emotions. But, he was trying.

12. I Wish They Share

Everyone thought I, Aiden William Melone, having everything going for me. I have a lovely wife, a great job, and two grown kids! Little do they know I am vexed by the challenging aspects of my family life. My kids cannot get over the fact that I am remarried, and I know it disappoints my wife Charlotte for not being accepted as a member as my "immediate" family. It hurts me to see Vera and George suffer from the loss of an intact family with their biological parents. It also pains me to witness how difficult it is for Charlotte to be in that awkward position a blended family could put one in. But surely, I wish they all can get along. I love them all too dearly to allow any friction to indicate anything other than my deepest love for each one of them. I avoid friction at all costs.

"Let's all go to a movie together." When Vera and George came visit together, I suggested all kinds of activities and planned dinners for the family.

"We rather go downtown and hit some music venues," proposed Vera firmly.

"We could. What do you like to do, George?" I had to make sure Vera didn't appear too bossy.

"We can go play golf during the day, and at night, we could do anything." George was up for anything.

"OK, we hit the golf course at 10:00 and go have some fun in the evening: music, movies, and all." I concluded.

I thought I had it all arranged perfectly and so was taken aback when Charlotte objected:

"I still have to work today and tomorrow. Why don't you three go ahead? I will only join you for an early movie."

"Good! You don't have to go," George announced quickly.

Detecting the tension in the air, I tried to smooth the ruffled feelings: "Oh, come on. Let all do things as a family."

"I only care if we get to see the bands I love in town." Vera expressed her nonchalance about being a family.

"If Charlotte doesn't want to go. Me and Vera get to be chauffeured around in the front seats. Hooray!" George threw in more acerbic comment.

I just had to give in. There was no point trying to persuade my disobedient wife and my rotten kids to do things together happily like a unified family.

Charlotte tends to be anti-social; she often excuses herself into her own study, especially when Vera or George is around. I don't understand why she can't be more welcoming.

"Why are you not going downtown with us?" I pulled her aside and asked.

"I thought I'd leave you three to spend some time together – only the three of you. I meant well. A movie together with your kids for me is enough. I do have an early start tomorrow." Charlotte explained.

I know that's not the whole story. Charlotte can either get involved or stay out of it. As far as I am concerned, she blocks out the kids more than they do to her. Doesn't George always come over to our house? Isn't Vera too lovely to avoid? Why can't Charlotte be grown-up enough to bond with my children?

I have talked to my kids and my wife separately on more than one occasion about sharing the love I have for them. I love Charlotte, I love Vera, and I love George. Loving any one of them does not take away my love for another.

Having to feel loved and get attention from me, Charlotte, Vera, and George are constantly vying for control of my devotion to them -- too much for one, too less for another, not enough this, not enough that….

George shows me his accomplishments or hurls off his irritation to engage me in his life:

"Dad, my single hits top 20 today."

"Dad, I am working with the biggest star in town."

"Dad, I just signed up to be a model."

"Dad, I have the biggest gig coming up. You've got to come see me."

"Dad, I got a hat-trick last night. You missed the game!"

"Dad, if you don't come to the next game, I am going to join another team."

"Dad, what the heck, I've been calling you all day. Why don't you answer your phone?"

....

Vera shares with me her opinions and the highlights of her life; she also makes demands from me, asks questions and seeks advice:

"Dad, don't you think this country's got to straighten up its justice system? Give them education, not punishment!"

"Dad, the best show to watch is on tonight. You've got to jump on the bandwagon."

"Dad, help me design my bookshelf."

"Dad, how do I fix my car?"

"Dad, what happens to Lord Gargor in the series? Isn't he supposed to be immortal?"

"Dad, you've got to send Aunt Susie some presents. Her birthday is coming, and her daughter just had another baby."

"Dad, you see how cute Nina is in the picture I sent you?"

"Dad, it's your priority to take care of your daughter's needs!"

. . . .

My wife Charlotte is more subtle, but I know I need to show her affection and appreciation. She wants to share a good life with me:

"Dear, look here the presents I got for your birthday."

"Addie, do you like this dress I am wearing?"

"Addie, how do I look?"

"Dear, who are you talking to so early on the phone?"

"Addie, you look great in that new shirt I got you."

"Dear, let's try out that new restaurant. I don't like going to the same restaurants over and over."

"Addie, why do you have to spend every weekend helping your relatives fixing stuff?"

"Dear, can't we do some traveling this holiday season?"

. . . .

I feel blessed by the love around me and feel satisfied when I show people how much they are loved. I love mankind and do not hold back whenever I can help people. I believe I often get love in return.

My wife Charlotte seems to be ambivalent about my generosity. She sometimes indicates that she'd rather spend some alone time with me than going out of our way to rearrange our plans for others. Although she is usually agreeable lending a helping hand, she appears also affected when too many petty chores take up too much of our time. I guess the reason why she feels ill at ease is because I am the one getting credit being the messenger of love, whereas she is frequently self-effacing, calling the shots behind the scenes. Yes, she calls the shots, alright! I mostly do what my wife wants us to do in our spare time.

What Charlotte doesn't understand is that I can't be blamed for being capable and popular.

"I have a lot of friends and relatives, and people like me. What can I do? I am the man!" I once said to Charlotte trying to explain why our weekends had to be spent solving others' problems.

"Being popular does not mean that you have to attend to other's whims all the time. You're well liked, I know. But, do people even know you, honestly?"

"Why, of course they know me! What do you mean by that?"

Charlotte can be too "complex" in her way of reasoning and thinking: "You have a big heart – a heart of gold actually. I love you for that, but you can't expect to please everyone and to be life of the party all the time."

"Why, of course everyone loves me!"

I believe in good karma and perform acts of kindness. Charlotte thinks I talk too much about myself. But the world is all about our projections of ourselves anyway. She just needs to be more social and express herself more. My dear wife can be shy; I will have to bring her out! I will have to have them all share!

13. What Goes Around Comes Around

What goes around comes around. Aiden's kids disregarded Charlotte, and Charlotte was not righteous enough to encourage amity or better rapport, either. The lack of connection created the biggest conflict in Aiden and Charlotte's life. Charlotte gave up on pleasing those children and turned a cold shoulder to them, while Vera and George were perfectly content not having to deal with Charlotte. Aiden, in the lackluster family dynamics, felt powerless and resorted to a laissez faire approach.

While righting all other people's wrongs, Aiden let family matters develop in their own courses, hoping miraculously his loved ones would someday develop the desirable bond themselves. It might take time; it might require drastic transformation for Aiden's immediate family to become more like a family. Or not.

For Charlotte, it was futile processing her resentful emotions and waiting for Vera and George to grow up. She was drained dealing with children, or young adults for that matter, the messes they made, the havocs they raised, the things they expected, and the constant needs for guidance and advice from her all-knowing husband.

"I need to get to the gig, and my car's broken down. Can you give me a ride?"

"I only eat Vegan food. Do not give me meats."

"My girlfriend is mad. What should I do?"

"Brandon is not happy at his job. Can you give him some directions?"

"I only see you when I visit. Take us shopping and then we want to have dinner at the Flannery Steakhouse."

....

Charlotte took George's girlfriends out to dinners to have one-on-ones when they encountered difficulties in their relationships with George.

"What's going on? What are you arguing about"?

"Everything. George didn't call to tell me he would come home at 5:00 in the morning. He just stood me up and posted pictures on social media with other girls."

"Did he tell you who they were? I suspect they're just his fans." Charlotte tried calming the girl down.

"No! He's always making excuses. They're not just fans or musician associates. He's so flirtatious!"

Charlotte played the peacemaker and tried instilling some "guy-Q" to whoever George's dating. However, she could do nothing right. George's relationships hardly grew to anything stable or solid. Charlotte could not advance anyone's maturity level. She just ended up being drained in others' drama

While Charlotte withdrew and refrained from playing any role in Aiden's children's lives, she still could not escape the "evil stepmom" label. Whatever she did or did not do, she was presumed and condemned as the cruel and pitiless woman with little love for her husband's children. Perhaps in some implausible way, she had a hand in designing her own suffering. Could she have done more or done less? One must take responsibility for one's own actions or inactions -- and not to place blame.

What will it take to become more mindful of one's behaviors or reactions toward other people? What goes into the process of building a healthier relationship? It was easier for Charlotte to pay no attention to the children who didn't want her in their lives, but it seemed imperative for her to recognize the need to be more involved, albeit how unwelcome or irrelevant her support was to those children.

It was a convoluted path for Charlotte to try and try again to help Aiden feel whole about his family. She was thoughtful and capable of contemplating for a better course for her marriage. However, this sort of insight did not come readily discernable. It was through observations or examples of other people the family members might come to a certain level of awareness.

"That's a lot of antagonism. You shouldn't become the enemy," suggested a good friend of Charlotte's, Tiffany Wilson.

"They treat me like an enemy. I would rather been seen as an OK stepmom, or any insignia other than an enemy." Charlotte protested.

"My parents were divorced. I often wished Daisy was not around when I spent time with my dad. I understand how Vera and George think." Harboring her own negative feelings for her stepmom Daisy, Tiffany often projected her own emotions unto Charlotte's marriage.

"I give them space …," muttered Charlotte, amazed at how adults or children alike, could be so blind to their own egocentricity.

"I can also imagine how hard it is for you. Just come have a spa day with me when Vera or George is with Aiden!" Tiffany offered.

"I have no problems letting them have their own time together. In fact, I like it when I get to have some 'me-time'." Charlotte was too independent to see "girl-time" as the remedy to her family dynamics.

In any case, Charlotte understood the attachment between Aiden and his children. She was not going to disrupt it, but hoped they recognized that she existed, and that change or restructuring of family was just part of life!

How come Charlotte could not have a healthy relationship with Aiden's children? She had seen stepmoms getting along just fine with their stepchildren. She had seen husbands including their wives along with their children in family matters. She had seen stepchildren celebrating their stepparents wholeheartedly without any reservation. But no, not for Charlotte, she could not even get a hug from Vera. Aiden had to be around to facilitate such an expression of warmth and turn their hug into a "group hug"!

Perhaps Charlotte just had to be big-hearted and tried harder. She remained amiable and awkward at the same time when Vera or George was around. And, her husband, was not the type of a delicate person to help dissolve the awkwardness. He was concentrated on being the greatest dad, and his immense love did not provide unwavering or constant assurance to soothe his own wife.

14. My Dad Is Under Charlotte's Spell

My dad is under Charlotte's spell, no doubt about it. He tells me to grow a big heart and regard her as my family. He holds out an umbrella readily to shelter Charlotte on her raining days. He opens car doors for her as if she were a regal queen. He listens to her ideas and commands like a puppy in heat. He takes her everywhere with him. He hardly has time for me anymore! I mean, who doesn't have time for me, for the marvelous George Melone,?!

How unfair it is to have some outsider intrude my family like that. I am supposed to be respectful to her for no reason other than she's married to my dad. I am supposed to do as she says, and I hate that.

"I don't want to sit in the back. My legs are too long for the backseat." I had to be crammed in the back seat when Charlotte was in the same car. I had no problems speaking out and requesting the front seat next to my dad.

"It's OK. You can have plenty of room on the left side. Why don't we trade seats?" My girlfriend Robin offered.

"Hey kids, we are going to have fun, so just enjoy the ride." Dad was super happy to have me and Robin along on the camping trip.

I bet no one can make Dad as happy as I can. I am the one who makes him proud; I share with Dad the same passions for music and sports. Charlotte is just a wife; Vera is such a goody two shoes in front of Dad that she can never be as cool as I am. I am the celebrated child. I live dangerously and Dad gets all the thrills from my daily reports. I update my social media constantly and I call Dad every day with the greatest news ever!

So how come Charlotte gets to bewitch Dad like that? How come I have to squeeze chunks of time in my busy life to call Dad, only to get delayed responses simply because Dad and Charlotte are "in the middle of" something?

Something -- Dad is always doing something with Charlotte. That one time I got to take Robin with me to their camping trip, it turned out to be the biggest disaster ever. It might be because Robin was constantly raising hells about me having girls' pictures on my cell phone and went off in the middle of the night to show how she could pick up and just leave me. It might be because I had to take Robin and her dog Monica to grocery shopping during the trip several time in a row. It might be I had to take care of Robin, Monica, and fight for time to spend with Dad. For whatever reason the trip went south, it was for sure, because Charlotte was there, too!

Charlotte bought a real nice gift for Robin and talked to her about being confident and giving me space and time. Charlotte told me to take Robin for a walk and to talk things out. Charlotte explained how difficult life could be if me and Robin couldn't communicate and work together on our issues. Charlotte played her uke and messed up the flow of me and Dad's duos. Charlotte hoodwinked Dad into regarding her as a fabulous wife! I am so sick of Charlotte!

I am fine with "Charlotte this and Charlotte that" in my life, but what I truly need is Dad's advice and support. That time, if Charlotte hadn't urged me to go out of my way to look for Robin, I could have gotten rid of Robin completely by now. Me and

Robin are just always on and off, on and off, and on and off again. I will be better off breaking clean!

Even Dad and Charlotte agree that I should not be tied down in an unhealthy relationship. I should find someone who is mature enough to be aware and be fine with the fact that I will have many girls' pictures and many more buddies and fans who I need to hang with. I get so tired answering Robin's questions and addressing her insecurities. I wish I can stop the relationship with Robin completely.

But for some reason, Robin just keeps coming back to my life. I need her driving me to a gig, and then she is back. I need to play with Monica and have a pet friend, and then Robin is back. Robin is back when I need to share the foods I cook. Robin is back when I have down time to roll with her and watch movies. Robin is back when she buys me expensive DJ equipment. Robin is back when she gives me birthday or Christmas presents. Robin is back when I need a "plus one" for various parties. Robin is back when I need to have a girlfriend. Robin is back when I feel like her company. Robin is back when I am sick. Robin is back when I find out she is dating other people. Robin is back after so many of my failed first dates. Robin is back when I ask her to. Robin is, Robin is back; she is back and back again!

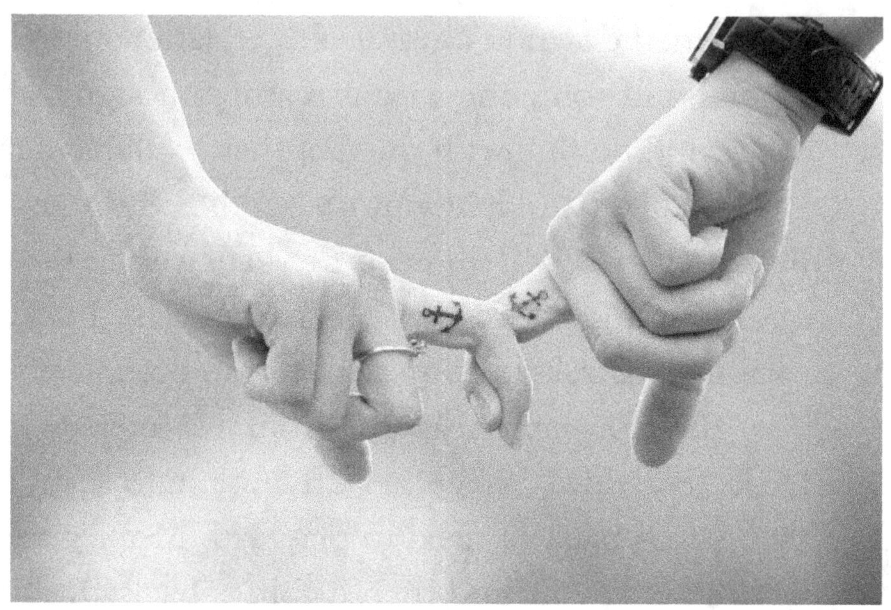

Now I kind of understand why Charlotte is so indispensable to Dad. Charlotte does take care of Dad although I blame her cooking -- it puts that big belly on Dad for real. Charlottes does provide different life experiences for Dad. Being such a smart-ass world traveler, Charlotte does make me curious sometimes -- I hate that they don't invite me to their various houses or get-away trips more often. Charlotte does look pretty when she wants to, although I will never mention that or let on about the fact that she's quite alright.

I now kind of realize why Dad is under Charlotte's spell. In fact, she bewitches him into neglecting the most important person in his life: me. She is just my dad's wife, and I am his blood! But I guess he needs his woman just as I need my girl. Robin does take up a lot of my time and energy. Dating does anyway. But still, who is to say when it comes to making decisions about Dad's life, Charlotte's preference should take precedence over mine!? Blood is thicker than water!

15. What About Me

I always thought I am the only one who can bring Dad infinite delight and joy. I call up Dad to share what I have accomplished in life. I make demands of him so that he knows he is always needed. I send him pictures of me, the fabulous Vera Davis, with Brandon and my cat Monica on my side. I brighten up my father's days. What more would Dad need in life to be happy?

"Dad, mail me some of those yummy coffee pods you got in your local specialty store. And here is my shopping list for you to fulfill. Get a pen and a piece of paper"!

"Not a problem. Just take pictures of the items you want." My dad likes to shop and fix things for me.

"And here is a pic of me taking Monica for a bicycle ride. Call me; I have time to chat now." Bonus to Dad's daily enjoyment!

"OK, we're in the middle of a movie. Can I call you in twenty minutes?"

What? My dad's life actually involves Charlotte? He should just talk to me when I call. He should just take the time to hear what I have to say!

I have the funniest stories to share and the best jokes to tell. Why does Dad rather wait till he and Charlotte finish the move? Why does he have to keep me waiting on a call back from him? What about me!?

I give my father lists of things to buy and chores to do, so that he feels needed. I do need him still. I need his advice on cars, home repairs, and career paths for me and Brandon. I need to borrow money to buy new stuff. I need to share with him details of my life, so that we are connected, and I remain the most fabulous person in his heart.

Now that I have to deal with Charlotte. That's so unfair. To think that I refer to Dad as "Charlotte's man" makes me want to puke. I wish she did not exist. I imagine in some ways that Charlotte becomes less smart and pretty. I wish to have nothing to do with her. But she always finds ways to situate herself right in front of me. It's just annoying.

When I try to solve crossword puzzles with my dad, Charlotte will come up with big words that no one else knows. When I think about my inheritance, I also have to take Charlotte's siblings, nephews and nieces into consideration. When I celebrate birthdays and holidays with my dad, Charlotte is simply there, an unwanted addition to my family. What?! Charlotte is family? Can Charlotte be family? Must I really call her -- family?

My aunt said to me that I was immature, not acknowledging Charlotte as whatever. Well yes, I was a sassy teenager, but I am not as feisty to Charlotte now. I even say hello to her on the phone when Dad prompts me to. I even think she is quite alright when she shows hospitality when I visit my dad.

What more do I need to do? I don't want Charlotte in my life. I don't want her to take away my time with my dad. I don't want to become too friendly with her. It really grosses me out to picture Charlotte with my dad. I am jealous of their life together.

But my dad's happiness is important to me, too. If he is happy with Charlotte, I will just put up with her. If he wishes me to be nicer to his wife, I will try to understand.

But that's about as far as I would go. I can't force myself to like her. I can't pretend that I don't miss having Dad all to myself. I can't say that I will ever feel that Charlotte is part of the family, period. Mom would always be number one and dear family, not Charlotte.

16. The Play

Despite the difficulties with Aiden's children, Charlotte was blessed in her matrimonial union with Aiden. They traveled a bit of the world together. They attended social gatherings, local performances, and sporting events. The plays, concerts, artistic events pertained to Charlotte's favorite pastimes, while Aiden's interests in athletics and music steered them to explore new pursuits.

At a little theater, some actor on the stage was delivering Beckett's lines:

"There's man all over for you, blaming on his boots the faults of his feet."

He then, looked at himself in a mirror and muttered more obscure words:

"I forgot to be a student; I am humbled now that I see clearly my own visage …."

It was discernable to Charlotte as to how the actor's soliloquies implied significance of the arts of self-expression, as well as powers of self-knowledge or self-criticism. She watched every change in the actor's facial expression and body movement, while Aiden's short attention span seemed to make him drift away to someplace else.

After the play, Charlotte asked Aiden: "It was great! Did you like the show?"

"It's OK. The stage looked splendid, but I almost fell asleep during the long monologues!" Aiden was usually drawn to the visuals and the sounds.

"Oh, those were great speeches delivered with passion! Such catharsis …."

"What catharsis," said Aiden with his eyebrows raised. "I can get more catharsis with walls of music!"

"Words have great power, combined with the theatrical effects, they provide abundant food for thoughts." Charlotte was more literary, and Aiden, musical.

Aiden's and Charlotte's tastes were quite different, but they generally enjoyed a variety of activities together. Charlotte found joy in arts and shared her interpretations in ways that might encourage Aiden to appreciate multifaceted levels of subtle artistic representations.

"The roles we play, the costumes and masks we wear, the arts we create, and the tales we tell others and ourselves -- are means to fulfill our quests for meanings and love," elaborated Charlotte.

"I got it. So we shouldn't blame outside factors for any dissatisfaction in our life conditions. What about doing our parts to make life better? How about saying yes to Vera and George?" Aiden inquired.

Here we go again – people can be so confined in their ways of thinking when projecting one's own affairs onto anything that takes place in their lives. For Aiden, everything tended to be viewed in its relations with his own children. Everything Aiden said or did, with or without Charlotte, circled back to his own fixation on his two kids. Other people existed only to validate their presence and glory.

Charlotte looked away incredulously. She recalled how George smirked and said to her: "Good luck with that. Let's see if my dad would go along with you when I tell him otherwise." George was right about his ability to sway his dad. The pressure and manipulation of Aiden's kids took such a heavy toll that it would eventually kill Charlotte.

17. Looking for Merits

There's no point trying to get Aiden to see how important it is not to say yes to every demand from Vera and George. Aiden's overcompensation to his kids does not help them grow. But by Jove, if anyone points that out to Aiden, he will side with his kids' conspiracy theory to imagine that everyone else is just sabotaging his relationship with his children!

I do agree that everyone must contribute to coexist peacefully. As his wife and life companion, I accompany Aiden to visit Vera quite often, and try to understand George's needs to constantly make phone calls to Aiden for advice or help. I gradually develop pity for Vera that is akin to an endorsement of the daughter's trifling entreaty for adoration, but George is a completely different story.

"Let's play Trivia and the loser has to buy dinner!" Vera suggested when Aiden and I visited her.

"OK. You're likely to have to spend money tonight then," assumed Aiden to his daughter.

"I don't believe so."

Vera tried very hard to come up with answers quickly and her competitive side was plain for all to see. She would bite her lips and shout out guesses that were sometimes over-the-top but hilarious. When asked which country invented chocolate, she yelled out: "Willy Wonka is from Britain .... No, it's Switzerland -- Swiss chocolate for Christmas!"

When Aiden revealed the correct answer, China, she argued: "China is for tea, not chocolate!" Vera fought till her face was bright red and insisted on conducting "fact-checking" on her cell phone before she would settle for an answer.

I saw at that moment in Vera, the determined focus of a bright mind. She is a lovable young woman striving to win every battle in her life. I pity her eagerness to prove her loyalty for her mom, as well as her aggressive and fearless defense mechanisms used to maintain her father's devotion for herself and no one else. Who am I to find fault with a child who is simply having a hard time coping with change in life? I wish she will grow in time; I am actually fond of her tenacity and fortitude. She is brave like her father! She is bashful in her own ways and outspoken like a bird constantly chirping for attention and recognition. She is very much like Aiden!

As far as George is concerned, I am just another steppingstone for him to attain his own stardom. He would use any resources available to him to gain support and reap attention or publicity. He says something sweet and nice and then turn around to stab me just when I catch a glimpse of his positive traits:

"I am so sorry I have been such a pain. I used to complain a lot and cause trouble for you. I promise I am all grown now."

"That's great! Be more responsible for your own existence, Buddy!" Aiden likes to be friends and play buddies with his own son.

"Duh, I am on my own, ain't I? Thanks to Charlotte I am not living with you anymore." George quickly makes his usual scathing comments.

Georg's words carry little weights or sensible meanings; he complains and complains about how his time is precious and everyone else should accommodate his schedule. He boasts about how his tastes are superb and could not be contaminated by non-vegan foods. He goes around smoking weeds and drinking bears like there's no tomorrow. He breaks whatever he touches wherever he goes, and concludes that "if he weren't such pain, it would not be fun for anyone around him"! George may think that being charming is enough to win people over, but only virtue and substance can communicate to souls. I am looking for merits to instill senses into my life with Aiden -- and that means a life with Vera and George in it.

Driven as he is to fame and wealth, George sometimes does delineate a persistently attention-grabbing personage. He could make Aiden feel so proud, and Charlotte, so ambivalent. Vanity has its way of articulating self-importance and haughtiness, urging others to home in on its narcissistic pride.

With narcissism, George shines through; with defiance, Vera shoves ahead. In any case, I wish I could find a way to be fine with their egocentrism, and perhaps to fight off affliction caused by my own emotional baggage. I wish I could have a life with Aiden that steers clear of tangled feelings and manipulations. But well, I cannot choose my relations; I cannot cherry-pick my husband's family, either. I must learn to coexist with them. I only hope that the bad name of an evil stepmother does not befall me. I am aware that all good and evil that comes upon me must be from myself. I must purge the troubled feelings within me!

18. Funny How Everyone Lost

Aiden continued to be the charismatic fun-lover and people-pleaser everywhere he went, but it was difficult for him to please everyone at home. He was stuck in between his kids and Charlotte, juggling with the love and care he had to give to each of them. Charlotte protested that Aiden's leniency toward his children affected their life together. Vera devised many a to-do-list or shopping errand for Aiden to maintain that bond with her. George wrecked havocs by his words and actions, or just simply mindlessly demanding attention from Aiden. It was ironic how everyone in Aiden's immediate circle was cranky about the immense love he so generously bestowed on the world. Was Aiden's love for everyone too wide-reaching? Was it too ubiquitous, and so appeared accidental and absent-minded, like a busy bee visiting a variety of plants to feed on them and provide them with the pollination services at the same time?

When you love your kids more than your spouse, everyone loses. Aiden loved his immediate family members equally in his own view, but subconsciously he often left Charlotte's needs unheeded. Little did he recognize that it's crucial to maintain the best relationship with Charlotte to help his own children.

"Give me your Christmas lists. I will go shopping for whatever you want." The first thing about holidays for Aiden was buying stuff for his kids.

"Last Christmas, I wanted a new car, but you didn't loan me any money," complained Vera.

"Well well, a car is a big purchase. How about items I can afford?"

For Vera and George, alas, the cup of Dad's devotion runneth over: merchandises bought; paternal duties performed. Aiden's dedication did not, however, benefit everyone. Vera and George were demanding and entitled; they ended up relying on Aiden for every little detail in their lives. Meanwhile, happiness and success of the family was sacrificed simply because Aiden and Charlotte were not in sync: he was overindulging, while she was an outsider to the Aiden-kids affiliation.

Aiden did not realize that while he deemed loving his kids natural and obligatory, he needed to also stick up for Charlotte. The latter required a conscious choice or constant reminder, at which Aiden was inept due to his propensity for male insensitivity. His children-before-spouse parenting mentality bothered Charlotte and made her feel distant from Aiden, let along Vera and George.

"Another shopping list? What about you, are your kids sending you any birthday presents?" Charlotte was taught filial obligations to her parents, while Aiden was habitually paying and providing for his children, even when the children were grown and should have been independent.

"I don't need anything from them; I told them not to send me anything," replied Aiden.

"You're such a pushover," muttered Charlotte. That was about all she needed to say to put Aiden in a foul mood, yelling and cursing for hours.

Charlotte was constantly struggling with wanting to be warmer toward Aiden's children and refusing to give in to their capricious demands. Aiden and Charlotte were hardly a team on that front -- they did not marry to spend a life together because of Aiden's children, but the children turned out to shape a very draining relationship that they had to deal with, separately.

Charlotte should have come first for Aiden. Their marriage, by itself, had enough of its own good and bad sentiments to last a lifetime -- and the dynamics among Aiden, his children, and Charlotte were difficult, to say the least. It just added to the challenges in a marriage.

Aiden as a husband, had a life to plan and live together with Charlotte, and the decisions they made as a couple did not always involve them kids. For Aiden, it was nearly impossible to leave his kids out of anything. For Charlotte, a healthy distance was much needed to help her cope. It wasn't that she did not hope to have a great family including Aiden's children; it was more like she couldn't expect Aiden's kids to see her as family. With limited expectations, she learned to accept the life with Aiden as it was. While she loved her husband to no end, their marriage was not without flaws. While he loved the whole world, he let his own wife feel taken for granted, like someone he did not need to tend to, someone who would always be around to love him.

19. We All Have to Do Our Parts

My stomach is in knots knowing no one in my immediate circle needs more love from me! Am I not giving so much attention already? How come my efforts go unnoticed? Charlotte protests that I don't communicate with her, and that I don't focus on building our life together. Vera thinks that she's adopted because I seem to give too much to George. George complains that I don't spend enough time with him, and refuses to understand how busy I am, and how I, Aiden Melone, married to Charlotte Melone, am also supposed to be with my wife.

I guess we all have to do our parts to make things right: I have to form alliances with Charlotte and be thoughtful. According to Charlotte's friend, Ms. Martin the expert, your spouse always comes first because he or she is the person you face the world together and share everything with: "You must form a united front. Kids can be manipulative if they know they can take sides."

I sometimes feel it is difficult to let my kids take anyone else's side but mine. I need their affection regularly as they need mine. I worry that if I don't bath them with devotion and care, I will lose their love for me. How pitiful that they should bear the pain of their parents' divorce!

I guess Charlottes must do her part, too. She needs to see how I cannot possibly expect Vera and George to be comfortable with a new woman in their father's life. She needs to compromise a bit to allow me to share our life with my kids. She's got a strong sense of herself, sometimes too independent and formidable to take any nonsense from my rotten kids!

As far as Vera and George are concerned, they only need to be civil to their father's wife, not making hurtful or caustic comments or behaving disrespectfully any chance they get. I can see how unbalanced and uncomfortable they are around Charlotte, too. Ah, those dear children of mine!

I ache for Vera and George, and I want to make Charlotte happy, too. I am stuck in between and always get reproached when anything goes wrong or if anybody gets sour about something. And that happen way too often. It doesn't seem like anyone's got enough love from me while I am trying all I can to be a good father to my kids and good husband to my wife. I wish they will see how hard it is for me. I wish they can get along with one another someday!

20. She Was No Doormat

Charlotte recognized that Aiden's children would behave better if she warmed up to them whether she ended up hurting herself in the process or not. She knew from the history of dealing with Aiden's children that, no matter what she did or how she acted, she would be hurt. She would be civil but refused to let them walk all over her. Children do best with authoritative parenting, and with high levels of cordiality and control at the same time. It's not that Vera or George was a kid anymore, but they both still needed the right mix of parenting modes -- since Aiden was nowhere near being authoritative when interacting with his grown kids, and Charlotte couldn't play any part in their lives, she could only try ensuring that she wasn't an easy prey for their manipulation. She stood up for herself when needed to.

Charlotte didn't know how to react to Aiden's kids at first; their insolence had shocked and hurt her so that she had been frozen, not knowing how to react to them.

"Why do I have to eat leftover? Is there anything fresh in this house?" George had complained about everything.

"That's no business whatsoever of Charlotte's; she doesn't need to be there." Vera had built a wall.

Maya Angelou famously said that you may forget what someone said to you, but will always remember how their words made you feel. Charlotte did not want to remember all the details of how she was treated or what those kids said. But she could not forget the burning sensation of embarrassment and humiliation. However, she was no doormat. She was not one to stay quiet when someone shouted insults or threw punches at her.

"That's why you need to cook for yourself, Boy." Charlotte was amazed at George's predisposition to think how others needed to serve him in any way he liked. She told him to make his own meals!

"When you say OK, then it should be OK!" Vera claimed that Aiden had the absolute power to determine everything for himself and Charlotte as a couple.

Charlotte needed to take control of her own life with Aiden. She made her point across:

"No, this weekend we're taking a road trip up in the mountains and therefore George can't come over to use his father's computer."

Vera wanted George to visit Aiden so that three of them along with her husband Brandon could play a video game together.

Vera tried to steer her father into attending to her needs over living his own life: "Not this weekend! I need you around to instruct Brandon how to fix the heater!"

Instances of Vera and George making Aiden and Charlotte rearrange their plans, made Charlotte cringe. She objected to rescheduling her plans and stood up for herself on more than one occasion. At times, she saw how Aiden was caught in between, she compromised but would not fall victim to any exploitation.

Against the backdrop of Aiden's permissive parenting, Charlotte's expectations about manners, scheduling, and respect appeared draconian and rigid. But she would not give in and allow Vera and George to be rude to her. Still, they didn't have any sense of what's wrong with their demands, no boundaries. They clashed with Charlotte and assumed that their dad would always go along with their requests over Charlotte's wishes.

21. Brandon and I Are Married

The time people in my branches of families were united and happy was when Brandon and I got married. I planned the whole wedding and brought together my mom's family, Brandon's family, Dad, and Charlotte. The love Brandon and I share may be the key to bond my disintegrated families. Brandon and I are marred, and my family can be happy.

"You're supposed to take me down the aisle. So, wear something color-coordinated to match me and Brandon." I reminded Dad.

"OK. Are you wearing Grandma's wrist lace?"

"Yes, but I need you to take it to a jeweler to polish it."

"How about the speech? Who is giving the speech?"

"Auntie Ann is doing the speech." I made sure Mom's family got to deliver the speech on my behalf.

I made sure Dad and Charlotte were sitting in the back, not prominently together with my mom's family. They could be in the back, especially Charlotte. She would not sit in the front and center with my mom's family. Besides, I am front and center anyway, on any occasion!

The wedding turned out to be fun for everyone in attendance. Even Charlotte seemed to have fun, talking to people about how she was just another adult in my support system. Perhaps, she isn't that bad after all. However, I still wish she had nothing to do whatsoever with my life, but she's Dad's wife. That is a fact I may need to take into consideration. How unpleasant!

22. Their Life in the Back Burner

It was the way Aiden put Vera's wedding front and center, too. He placed the picture of Vera and himself all dressed up in wedding getups, front and center, in the house where he lived with Charlotte. Being the proud father of the bride, he praised and announced how beautiful and grown-up Vera was. What he overlooked was his own wedding with Charlotte. He never mentioned or discussed his own wedding in detail -- by self-effacing, he was hiding the guilt he felt about how Vera and George had to live through his failed first marriage and his wedlock with Charlotte. The pledge to Charlotte was always in the back burner.

"I want this to be about Vera, not anyone else's drama." Aiden warned Charlotte how important it was for Vera's wedding to be successful.

"I will just be quiet," replied Charlotte.

On Vera and Brandon's wedding anniversary, Aiden would say to Charlotte: "Let's send something to surprise them. Let them know we're thinking about them!"

"Go ahead. Go send another care package." Charlotte let him be.

Aiden was happy with Charlotte when his kids were taken care of.

"Look at all the vegan dishes Charlotte made for you." Aiden exclaimed while George spent Christmas with them one year.

"...." George said nothing.

"Let me take a picture and send it to Vera!" But Aiden was in heaven when Charlotte "did her part," and he had to share with his daughter right away.

Another year, while George was visiting during Christmas, Charlotte requested that he took care of his own stomach and watch out for his veracious drinking.

"Going through 48 bottles of beers in a day is not normal. Tell George not to drink like a fiend. And he can do his own cooking if he only complains about what's served on our table." Charlotte insisted.

"He can do his cooking; he can do whatever he wants." Aiden let George do "whatever."

"You need to lay down the rules and teach him to become more responsible." Charlotte spoke her mind.

"Yes, thanks for all your support." Aiden went on scowling anytime Charlotte had to say something about his kids.

"I love you unconditionally." Aiden would say to Charlotte when she gave in, which permitted George's reckless behavior to perpetuate and Vera's whims to be indulged.

Aiden was cheerful and chatty as a bird when playing online video games with Vera, George, and Brandon. He would seek any ways or means to feel connected with his kids. Charlotte grimaced while the four adults shouted and ululated while dodging some bullet in the fantasy video-game world.

23. I Am Always in Trouble

It's so strange that I am always in trouble, with Charlotte around. I can't do this, and I can't do that. Who is she to nag at my dad to "straighten me up"? George Melone doesn't need no straitening up. I should be able to do whatever I want and whenever I like. But I have to call first before visiting with Dad; I have to announce myself; I have to have permission …. Charlotte is just a royal bitch!

I am pissed at Charlotte for taking my time away from Dad. I wish she would just drop dead. If Dad leaves her for my sake, that would be the happiest day of my life. No one should tell me what to do, not even Dad. I am on my own now and I don't need lectures. I don't need permissions to do anything I choose to do, how I do it, and when I do it. Everyone should just get out of my hair!

That Charlotte causes lots of problems. I have to wait to schedule time with Dad; I have to pay for my own beers; I have to cook for myself now; I have to keep quiet when she is working. Why doesn't she just keep her opinions to herself?! Well, why can't I just drop by to visit? -- I guess I have to be more conscious of the consequences of not heeding rules. I would just get more shit from Dad.

24. One Bad Gene

One bad gene can permeate into an entire family like a worm inside you eating away nutrients bit by bit and eventually ruin the wholesomeness of your body. The bad gene in George, for example, affected the whole family, particularly when the family got together.

"I want to go have a bike ride." George declared before he had anything to eat one fine morning during Christmas.

"OK, please be careful not to hurt yourself or wreck the bike." Aiden reminded him.

"Avoid driving across the field, please." Charlotte offered.

"Why? Why should I listen to you?" George snapped.

Nothing was ever right between Charlotte and George. One would say something, and the other would take offense, by design or not. It was a pain to have any interaction.

"What are you making for Dad?" George asked.

"Just some chili," replied Charlotte.

"Oh, leftover again. I thought you're making something fresh."

"Chili tastes better the next day."

"That's silly."

Little conversations like that would trigger frictions and arguments. Every little detail in daily life seemed hard with these two in the same house. George made a mess everywhere and made asinine comments. Charlotte wished he would watch his own words and actions.

The conflict between the two never ended well: George was not allowed to just pop in the house to visit; George caused more trouble intentionally; Charlotte hardly felt like doing things for George; George railed against Charlotte continuously. The vicious circle went on. The entire family struggled, quarreled, adjusted, compromised, and then struggled, quarreled, adjusted, compromised, again and again ….

Some people bring out the worst of each other. In Aiden's mind, the tension between Charlotte and George (or Vera) was nobody's fault; it was just what it was. Aiden never thought about mediating; he assumed all would turn out OK if he kept showering everyone with immense love.

25. The Best of the Bunch

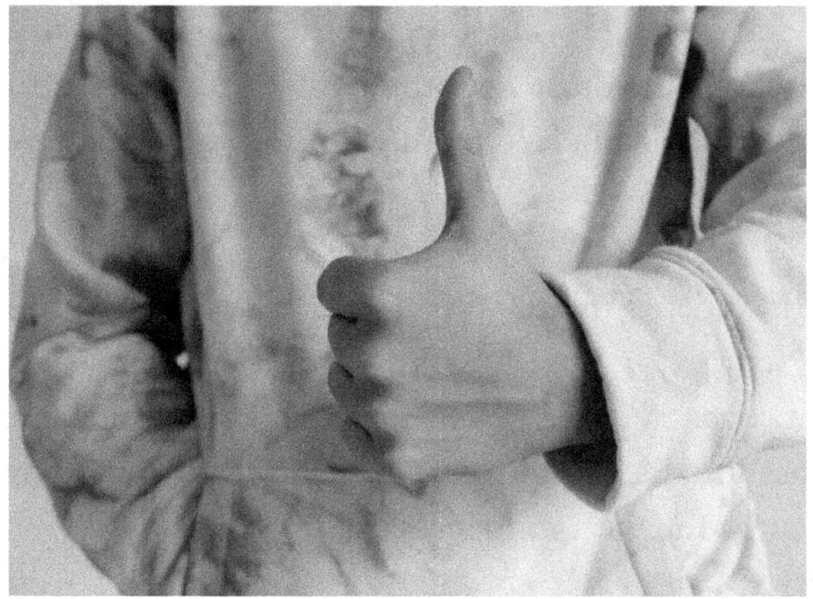

Aiden, by far, was the best of the bunch. He was the focal point that tied the family members together; he played a core role at his job and his community; he was the heart of all operations, private or public.

"I will cut the vegetables." Aiden would offer to help knowing Charlotte refused to prepare a vegan holiday meal just for George.

"I will say you can drink as many beers as you want if you pay for them yourself." Aiden tried getting George to realize how his drinking had a "price."

"I sent my co-worker a guitar for Christmas. He has been wanting to learn forever." Aiden took care of his buddies at work.

"I will pitch in. Let's buy a nice present for the chief." Aiden thought about his boss and colleagues.

"I bought our gardener a new machete because he broke his while cutting our trees." Aiden thought about everybody.

People loved Aiden. He loved them back. There was not a single person in the entire world who would not get along with the man with immense love.

However, no good deed goes unpunished. Aiden's immense love was destined to suffer a backfire as the family members in his immediate circle required more of his devotion. His kindness toward others seemed overzealous and self-validating. There needed to be differentiation and boundaries for spousal love, parental love, family love, and all other kinds of brotherly or sisterly bonds he established in his life.

As a parent, Aiden had a unique opportunity to teach his children how to have a healthy, secure attachment to him. By being a responsive caregiver, he needed to gauge the level of his interactions with his children that it allowed for the kids higher social functioning in life. How much of indulgence should one permit for one's children? What support and love should be given to one's spouse so that a couple can face the world together, and stand up against all odds as a united front? Aiden had much to learn, and Charlotte had yet, more to forego!

26. A Master Mischief-maker

Aiden's upbringing might have contributed to the making of a man with immense love, who sympathized with people around him and indulged his own children to no end. Youngest among his six siblings, Aiden had been running errands for his parents and his brothers/sisters to earn his keep. He had played with old toys, sports gears, and donned over-sized clothes -- hand-me-downs from his older siblings. He had managed and took care of various animals around the house all by himself: twelve dogs, five cats, ten iguanas, and six rabbits. Those animals had kept Aiden company more than others in the family as his parents had been busy trying to make ends meet and his older brothers and sisters considered him too young to hang with.

You're mistaken if you assume that the ardent young Aiden had followed orders or rules set by his much older siblings, or by his parents, teachers, and neighborhood elderly. Aiden had been a little playful and mischievous rascal as a young child!

"Aidee is causing trouble again, Mom! He fed carrots to the dogs and gave dogfood to the rabbits!" Aiden's older brother Todd had found those animals looking weird with wrong kinds of food residues on them, in their feed pans, and all over the floor.

"I didn't! I just taught all of them how to share their foods!" Aiden had believed that all people and animals should develop comraderies by sharing and loving one another.

Aiden had gotten a good lashing; 16 impressions had been made by his father's strap on his legs. Aiden had wanted his animal friends to befriend one another! And so that sort of punishments had not changed one bit of Aiden's enthusiasm for good fellowship among animals and humans alike.

"Aidee got called to the Principal's Office today; he broke his classroom window!" Aiden's sister Susie had reported to their parents.

"What's wrong with you? Why did you break the window?" Aiden's father had interrogated.

"I was playing with a ball. Nothing's wrong."

"What makes you think the classroom is the place to play balls?!"

When it's school trouble, the beating had doubled, tripled, and quadrupled. Aiden's uncle had been the school principal, and little Aidee had often been made an example to show how the school administration had tolerated no misbehavior! The bruises on Aidee's arms and legs had meant for all school children to see and to learn lessons from.

Aidee had completed tasks and carried out numerous chores for his parents and older siblings faithfully. His unwavering love had only strengthened after many a whipping -- to him, corporal punishment might not have made him obey rules, but it had made him a man, a tough kid taking all the straps for others. And, the examples he had set had been rewarding and worthwhile. He had been the most popular kid on the block. He had loved to have company, and others had loved to hang out with him! He had been willing to do anything for his parents, siblings, friends, and neighbors. He had desired approval from everyone and felt honored to help people in any way.

"Aidee, I bet you can run to the store and get some candy for us in ten seconds, much faster than me!" His older brother had tried to get Aidee to do things by praising and encouraging him. Little Aidee had been gung-ho for any kind of games or bets!

At Grade 5, Aidee and his buddies had often frequented an abandoned church in the neighborhood. They had "scored" all sorts of merchandise from junk yards of drugstores, grocery stores, and department stores: a three-legged sofa propped with a makeshift rod, a paint-stained rug big enough to sleep twenty kids, two rickety tables to set drinks and cigarettes on, and three pieces of lumber to form a triangle for a play area. Aiden and his friends had had lots of parties at that abandoned church; it had been a place for fun, enjoyment -- and friendship-building or prank-making.

Aidee and his friends had partied into the wee hours on a fine Saturday night. They had chatted about girls, sports, tricks and jokes on bullies, and everything under the sun.

"I dare you to ask Sharon out! Man, the most beautiful girl in the world." Aidee's buddy Jonathan Lee had challenged.

"I already did." Aidee had been always ahead of others, in thinking, in action, and in making mischief.

"How did you do that? Did she agree to go out with you?"

"Of course, she did! I showed up with little paper hearts in a basket with my mom's home-made cookies I know Sharon loves."

"Oh yeah, that's romantic but a bit lame. You should let her know you're a man."

"I know. I also held a cigarette in my hand when I gave her the basket." Aidee had been the perfection combination of a good bad boy.

"Alright! Let's see who can puff off the meanest smoke rings!" Someone in the group had suggested.

About twenty boys had gathered in the triangular play area for the competition. They had smoked and cracked jokes and forgot about the time. They had brain-stormed ideas for impressing girls, for winning a sport game, and for gaining life wisdom.

"A sailor was drowning in the sea. A ship came by, and he was offered a lifeboat. He said he didn't need the lifeboat because God would save him. Another whaler came along and attempted to pull him out of the water. He stayed afloat because he believed God would save him. Yet another trawler passed by him as he waited for God to rescue him. He died eventually, wondering why God did not save his life…." Aidee's buddy Christian Tower had often told stories to engage the bunch in "philosophical thinking."

"The moral of the story is that you should grab opportunities as they come instead of waiting for bigger and better prospects." Tommy Harris had suggested right away.

"Do not procrastinate!" Jude Norburn asserted.

"Never wait for Godot!" Aidee had been the clever and mischievous one.

"Nope, it means that God does not exist!" Nick McGowan the atheist had announced loudly.

"A teenage girl brings her boyfriend home to meet her parents. His haircut, his tattoos, his piercings are appalling to her parents. The mom says that he doesn't seem nice, and the girl disagrees, saying: 'Oh, he is nice otherwise he wouldn't be doing 500 hours of community service!'" Terry Malusa had told another joke.

"Yeah! Always look on the bright side!" Aidee's had cheered in jest, commiserating with the bad boy.

"I used to play spin the bottle in Grade 4. A girl would spin the bottle, and if the bottle pointed to you when it stopped, the girl could either kiss you or give you a nickel. See, that's why I am super rich now." David White had laughed at his own bad luck with girls in a very sarcastic way.

"When you have the money, you will have the honeys! Don't worry." Aidee had encouraged David, sounding like an experienced dater.

"I ask my cousin Liam when his birthday was. He says, 'February 20.' I ask him what year. He looks at me dubiously and says, 'Every year, man!'" Dan Hopp had been incredulous about Liam's short of all his faculties.

"Don't underestimate a youngster's mind. He makes every birthday count!" Aidee had advocated Liam's fresh outlook.

Young Aidee had sought out the good in all things and all people. But as a master mischief-maker, he had been also keen to place pranks on his friends. He had brought firecrackers with him and set them off using his buddies' lit cigarettes!

"Bang pop crack!" The firecrackers had sounded like hailstorms in the abandoned church.

"Woohoo! Give me more to play!" Every boy had been excited to stir up a roar.

"Bang pop crack!" "Bang pop crack!" "Bang pop crack!" ....

The whole place had been full of noises and laughers. Suddenly, someone had shouted: "Fire, Fire, Fire!" Another had screamed: "Let's go, let's go! The sofa is on fire." And yet another shrieked: "The whole place is full of smoke and fire now!"

The boys had run out of the church, finding no water sources anywhere. They had fled the church, realizing they could not have controlled the burning of combustible objects in the church. The fire had been spreading madly and the abandoned church, ablaze with colors that had been so vibrant that people had seen the fire from miles away. Hot flames had shimmered and appeared intense yellow, vicious orange, dazzling red, and other sorts of shades that had been too eerie to name.

Young Aidee had got into the vintage Mustang borrowed from his older brother Todd Melone and had driven away at top speed. Little had he anticipated its century-old brake to bust. He had tried so hard to slow down the car to no avail. He had ripped through the city streets as fast as lightning, screaming all the way.

Many passersby had witnessed young Aidee with a distorted face, turning as pale as a piece of white paper, while peculiarly still maintaining his handsome posture on that grand old automobile, looking like a radiant, luminous divine being. Aiden had been famous and widely admired since his boyhood!

27. They'd Come for the Boys

The police had inspected the surroundings of the abandoned and singed church. They had looked over how the uninhabited old church had caught on fire. They had gotten word that a bunch of boys had made the place their regular hangout. They had come for the boys.

"I don't know. We were there one day. The next day we went back, the church was in ruins!" Terry Malusa had completely copped out on the incident.

"People in the neighborhood said that they heard firecrackers going off in that church. Were you there playing with bottle rockets, son?" Officer Shepard had inquired.

"That was long time ago, sir. It wasn't when the church caught on fire." Jonathan Lee had fabricated.

"Who else was there?" Shepard had intended to interrogate more.

"I don't remember." Nick McGowan had feigned ignorance.

"We were playing outside, not inside. All of us!" Elusive as ever, David White had kept it vague and sarcastic.

"Who were 'us'?" The officer had sought more names.

"All of the boys in the neighborhood, sir." The same old David White had spoken irreverently.

Officer Shephard had not been able to get anything out of the several boys he had interviewed. He had enlisted more help from his precinct to go around the neighborhood to search for evidence. He had asked around for people to volunteer information. The neighbors had pretty much brushed the police off. No one had cared about the abandoned church anyway -- no one had had any desire to see any of the boys getting in trouble. The police had been given the cold shoulder and ceased all investigation. On the other hand, Aidee and other boys, just about twenty of them, had been allowed to redecorate the church and made it into their fantastic lair again!

28. Hockey Fights

Fast cars and fireworks had presented only a small percentage of the mischiefs the young Aidee had been up to. He had also had a proclivity for fights, especially during hockey games which he had started playing at age 3. He had got into a fight protecting his dog, Arnold, from the neighborhood bullies. He had gotten into a fight defending his championship in a school sport meet. He had gotten into a fight contending that he had been right about a debatable topic. He had gotten into a fight competing with other boys for a desirable girl. Mostly, he fought with his rivals at hockey games.

"What makes you think you can cross-check me!?" Young Aidee had shouted at the top of his lungs and lunged at a player.

Receiving the punches unexpectedly, the player had squealed in pain and fought back: "Ah, Ahhh! You want to fight?" He had yelled and hit Aidee in the chest.

Aidee had raised his forearms to block the strikes, slipping to the side like a wild animal dodging a hunter's bullets. He had gotten back on the offensive and pressed his opponent down and away, catching his torso, and rolling him unto the ice. But Aidee's rival had been no weakling; he had struggled to get back up on his feet, in a state of semiconsciousness, watching Aidee clenching his fists in slow motion. Aidee had acted promptly to maintain his lead and reached under the boy's elbow to tackle his waist and prevent him from regaining his sentience.

Aidee's foe had absorbed the trauma from the attack on his waist, suppressing the pain and kicking his way quickly back to the standing position. He had shifted to the left, only to meet Aidee's deadly right cross. Aidee had continued to punch and broken the boy's ribcage -- 2 of his ribs had been fractured. That had been enough to send the boy falling to the ice again, screeching and bleeding with excruciating pain.

Also badly bruised, Aidee had had all his ribs intact and 1 broken tooth. He had regarded pain as just an elusive feeling that his mind had been capable of taking in. Aidee had hold himself steady, standing upright and straight to face any enemies in any encounters.

While the two boys had engaged in a fierce match, pushing and striking each other. Other players from both teams had joined the two fighters. Most of the players had ended up scuffling, tussling, and clashing with one another. A heap of bodies had piled up on the ice rink, all tangled up and wound together like knotted coils.

The referees had come running to the mound of boys writhing on the ice.

"Cut it out! Cut it out!"

" No scrapes!"

The squirming boys had not heard any loud announcements from the referees. They had kept struggling with one another and quite a few of them had bled all over the ice. The rink had appeared crimson in some places and grimy in others. The audience had cheered so deafeningly that the sky had seemed to be lifted open -- although the spectators had been consisted of mostly friends and families of the players, they had been extremely vociferous.

The game had ended with Aidee breaking the tie in a shootout. Countless games had had similar scenarios. The fights, the tight competitions, and the persistent resolves to win had perpetuated into Aiden Melone's adulthood, even prolonging into all aspects of his life. Aiden's fought for his wins tenaciously in games, romances, careers, and family lives in various stages. He was a fighter, with the will, courage, ability, determination, and disposition to toil, battle, and go for the prizes he wanted. His focus was laser-sharp; his preparation was ample; his work was done punctiliously. His triumph in any facet of life was earned and well deserved.

29. Aidee Is Dead

"Aidee is dead! Aidee is dead!" Christian Tower had run all the way from Aidee's father's garage to Aidee's girlfriend's house.

"What do you mean 'Aidee is dead'? What happened?" Evalyn Beischel had inquired, puzzlement adding to her frustration. At age 12, one year senior to her boyfriend Aidee, she had looked like a full-grown beauty queen of 18.

"I just came from Aidee's house. His father was underneath the Mustang fixing the brake. I didn't see him. I didn't see him!" Christian Tower had been out of breath, gasping with fear.

"Calm down! Tell me what happened." Evalyn Beischel had commanded.

"Oh, I was telling Aidee about Jude Norburn's new supply of booze. I was so excited to have access to Jude's cabinet of Bourbon, Rye Whiskey, Scotch Whisky, Canadian Whisky, Tennessee Whiskey, and Irish Whiskey! I completely put Aidee's life in danger.

His dad heard everything. I am sure his dad's killed him already!" Ashen with anguish and terror, Christian had supposed that Aidee had been beaten to death for his expected attendance at a suggested drinking party!

"Get hold of yourself, silly." Evalyn Beischel had not assumed the worst.

"Aidee's dead! Aidee's dead already!" Convinced of the foreseeable punishment upon Aidee because of his own wrongdoing and recklessness, Christian Tower had repeated his thought and prediction.

"I'll go to Aidee's house and see what's what." Evalyn had decided quickly.

Evalyn Beischel had arrived at Aidee's garage and found him Alive and conversed incessantly with his father, Ryder Benjamin Melone. Ryder Melone, still lying under Todd Melone's Mustang, had sounded sonorous. He had bellowed every word he had uttered across the whole neighborhood. Aidee had also roared with embarrassment; his mortification had matched his father's wrath.

"I wasn't going to any drinking party, Dad!" Aidee had reassured his father.

"You'd better not cause any more trouble!" Thunderous commands had been Ryder's Melone's means of delivering his teachings to his sons, especially the master mischief-maker, Aidee Melone.

"I am not causing any trouble. I just learned how to fix the brake line, bleed the brake, and keep the system functioning well!" Aidee had been pleased about his newly acquired skills and prided himself on becoming an auto mechanic!

"I'm going to talk to Jude's father and see to it that you boys don't get to his liquor cabinet!" Ryder Melone had been known for his strictness, stubbornness, and authoritative doctrines. He had been also effective in organizing community meetings with other parents to discipline their children.

"Alright! We're not planning any drinking bash!" Aidee had avowed.

Instead of addressing Aidee, Ryder Melone had gestured toward Evalyn: "Evalyn, come on in now! You make sure there's no more shenanigans!" He had counted on Aidee's girl to keep the boy in line.

"For sure, Mrs. Melone! You don't have to worry about those boys drinking. They've been grounded for months since the church fire!" One year senior to the boys, Evalyn Beischel had acted the part.

"Don't … Evalyn, don't mention the church." Aidee had been jumpy, nervous about any reminiscence of the church fire that had enraged Ryder Melone to the point of no redemption.

"Now, you zip your month, Aidee. Go wash up and get Evalyn something warm to drink!" Stern as Ryder Melone had been to his sons, he had always behaved like a gentleman to girls or women.

"Ok, Dad. I'll do that. Thank you for all the work on the car!"

Young Aidee had behaved particularly well after Christian Tower's visit to his father's garage. He had appreciated the fact that Evalyn had come to his rescue. He had stayed in to help around the house.

He had been courteous to his siblings. He had obeyed his teachers at school. He had gone 4 months without being flogged and punished for some mischiefs he had cooked up. And, he had been alive and well!

30. A Little Indispensable Worker

As a matter of fact, Aidee Melone had conducted himself so well that he had been able to get a job as a barback at a local bar. At age 11, Aidee had grown tall and passed as a young adult. He had lied about being 18 and become indispensable at the bar.

"Aidee, please refill the icebox and all the liqueurs."

"Aidee, please run the dish washer and supply clean glasses."

"Aidee, please mop the spills in the bar area."

"Aidee, please help me move the empty bottles."

"Aidee, please get more napkins from the storage room."

For every request the bartender, Ethan Kasprak, had made, Aidee had fulfilled with efficiency and competence. The customers had noticed the friendly kid and liked him. They had come back to the bar wanting to witness the tall boy cracking jokes, showing off party tricks, or just receiving high praises from Aidee to make themselves feel fine and dandy.

Aiden had proved himself to be a natural salesperson with charismatic traits. He had been a little indispensable worker. He had been like a magnet attracting men, women, boys, and girls to revisit the bar. People had seen a diligent and good-humored boy, all wits and no angsts. They had loved to chat or play with him because he had possessed endless hilarious stories to tell and even more games to play. Little had they been told about the young Aidee's many hidden talents. It had taken Aidee seven more years of playing the guitar with his parents and siblings before he had officially become a professional performing musician!

31. Music Career

Aiden William Melone had been playing music professionally at local venues starting at the age of eighteen. He had excelled at singing and guitar playing after many practice sessions with his family. He had developed a love for rock and roll, rebelling against Ryder Benjamin Melone's country tunes. He had formed a rock band with his brother Todd Melone and some famous local prodigies in their twenties. He had had tons of fun hanging out with music lovers and rocking his way to the realm of sublime glory endowed by artistic endeavors.

At times, Aiden's performances had been entertaining; other times they had enlightened the audience in unanticipated ways and resonated long after the melodies had ceased.

"Wow, wow! That's a stunning tune you just sang. Did you write that song yourself?" A girl with long dark curly hair had asked Aiden, her bohemian multi-colored dress so long and wide that it had rustled through the dimly lit corner to make a grandiose appearance in front of the band.

"Yes, I wrote the song when I was 15, heart-broken, missing my first love who'd moved to another town."

"Oh, that's so disturbing and harmonious at the same time. How did you do that?" The girl had been visually moved by the piece.

"Well thank you. I am glad you enjoyed it."

Aiden's song had been visible as it had torn through every inch of the performance space like a wounded beast, only to become synchronized by the drumbeats, the guitar solos, and the bass themed chorus, tamed to a peaceful respite. It had climbed and climbed to a cacophonous crescendo and then fallen gradually to a symphonic diminuendo. It had made the audience stand up and move along with the rhythms. It had guided the audience to follow the hand gestures and body movements of the band members, raising their arms up high, clapping along with the beats of their own emotional pulsations.

"How should I put it? Your song made me sad and happy at the same time. I was transported into a state of quiet liberation." Another had commented encouragingly.

Under the influence of the band, the audience had felt empowered to deal with their own losses and hurts. With the music still reverberating in their ears, they had joined the musicians to tell and retell the stories. When the band's performance had ended, they had acknowledged their own desperate desire for the exact kind of cleansing brought about after facing injuries, sufferings, and lacerations, all the things that had wakened their minds and made them yearn for new horizons in life. They had bought the band's CDs and played them so repeatedly that their stereos practically had broken down under the strain.

Aiden Melone's song, "The Girl in Another Town," had created lasting effects on people, so had the artist's visage of sincerity and authenticity. The band had also presented other hit songs: "Apple Pie and Tree," "Rosemary's Garden," "A Dog Named Arnold," "Papa's Got a New Chainsaw," "My Mama Said," "Fish in the Creek," "Big City Boy," and "Grasshoppers in a Loop," -- to name a few. Aiden and his band members had turned little things in their rural surroundings into something sophisticated with an urban or universal feel. They had narrated splendid tales that people had related to, in rock ‘n roll style that had been so fresh and captivating.

Aide has been lucky enough to be able to make a living singing and playing in bands. He had built a group of loyal fans. He had traveled far and wide to perform on stage. He had collected hundreds of guitars and other instruments. He had made great friends and eminent contacts along the way. His teenage years up to mid-twenties, had painted a memorable picture – Aiden, as a young man, had had a successful music career. But that career had not lasted. Aiden Melone had quit performing after numerous late nights and long trips, realizing he had had the responsibility to stay home for Vera Melone and George Melone. Vera and George had required Dad to change career completely!

32. Shaping Up Well

Aiden Melone had switched to sales in healthcare computer software at the age of 28. He had joined his buddy Jonathan Lee to expand the company business to the south. He had moved his whole family south to be immersed in the local markets. Within a year in sales, Aiden had become the number one salesman and earned the title of "Employee of the Year." He had lived up to that title and shaped up really well in the business world.

But within a year, Aiden Melone's family had also split up. Cina had turned into a housewife who had had too many parties and expenditures -- too little solemnity or sobriety. Aiden had moved out and rented an apartment from the Kung Fu master from the Far East with Vera and George. Yes, during their "Bruce Chen Years," the kids had been happy training under the Kung Fu master, and Aiden had continued to thrive as a business man.

Aiden had raised his two kids single-handedly although he had often been away from home on business trips. His maid, Maria Santos, had helped with cleaning, cooking, and babysitting. The kids' mother, Cina, had visited and taken them to the house Aiden had left her. Vera and George had gone back and forth in between their parents' separate housings. Things had been looking up in Aiden's household, with a father earning money and providing for his family. Things had, on the other hand, developed into a downward spiral in Cina's world.

Cina had been drinking and using drugs heavily. She had been hardly sober to be a wife, a mother, or a rational person. Aiden had moved Vera with him to a different city further down south to take charge of his company's operations in that area. George had been relocated to live with his mother. From then on, Vera and George had alternated their living places a dozen times, until the divorce of their biological parents had been finalized.

Aiden Melone had climbed the corporate ladder at his sales jobs. He had successfully developed Jonathan Lee's company into the deep south. He had moved on to bigger and better firms. He had grown company revenues and built extensive networks. He had evolved as a businessman at work and artist at heart. He had always been a man with immense love, with enigmatic abilities to connect with babies, kids, young adults, people of his own age, elderly seniors – of both sexes, and with all kinds of animals, all sorts of high arts and low arts. Aiden Melone had been shaping up well, well into his middle-aged years.

33. Their Middle-Aged Romance

Aiden Melone and Charlotte Lewis had met each other more than one year prior to their courtship. The first time they had met up, Aiden had had a sleek gamboge-colored dress shirt on, earnest to impress. He had also put on a pair of odd off-white tennis shoes that had appeared too awkwardly mismatched with his fashionable top. He had advanced into his forties like cherished aged wine, comfortable in his own skin though showing a bit of belly fat.

Charlotte, on the other hand, had looked like twenty-eight in her early forties when she had made Aiden Melone's acquaintance. She had moved down south after divorcing her first husband. She had lost a bit of girlish shine and simplicity, and had aged well like a bewitching and enchanting piece of retro art, fully capable, self-sufficient, and primed to take care of herself while having the time of her life. She had materialized in Aiden's life -- an beautiful and young-looking woman, sweet, fun, mature, and intelligent.

"Wow, you look twenty! Are you sure you're only four years younger than me?" Aiden had exclaimed.

"Yes, sure. It's in my genes. I don't look my age." Hoping to live more fully and wisely with each passing year, Charlotte had not felt overly flattered. Aiden's compliment had sounded like a remark from any passersby attempting to hit on her.

Aiming to please, Aiden had continued: "You look so good. Nice dress! Let's go have dinner together."

"Maybe next time. I have other engagements." Charlotte had not felt enthralled by Aiden's excessive praises. She had wanted to keep the first date short.

Perhaps the milieu had been off. Sitting with a middle-aged tall and handsome guy in a mismatched outfit at a café had not turned Charlotte's crank. The admiration received had seemed too superficial to make Charlotte tick. Aiden had been nice-looking, but a bit peculiar, and so Charlotte had decided quickly to sidestep. She had chosen to slide into middle age with grace, taking time for herself instead of repeating relationship mistakes.

This first impression is crucial but is not always accurate. Judgment is generated by one's experiences and environments. But experiences accumulates and environments change, and so first impressions may evolve and transform as well. Charlotte had eventually realized her own misstep in trying to sidestep and avoid repeating her previous mistakes. Her first impression of Aiden had been unfair -- Aiden had not been a superficial, tasteless, and outlandish salesman. He had turned out to be a genuine, kindhearted, and persistent man! Charlotte had made presumptions like Jane Austen's protagonist, Elizabeth Bennet, who misjudges Mr. Darcy and puts herself in the predicament of hasty judgments. Indeed, Charlotte had had lots of pride and prejudice!

Aiden had not heard back from Charlotte for fourteen months straight, but it had not stopped him from trying to reconnect with her. He had thought himself deserving of a good woman after all those crazy and anxious years, building a sales career and supporting his kids. His hectic life had given way to the social whirl of teenagers but had slowed to a calmer pace. Taking his belt out a couple of notches had not made Aiden Melone lose his confidence.

"Howdy, Charlotte! This is Aiden Melone. I was just calling to see how you've been!"

"Oh, Aiden. Long time no see! I am just fine. How are you?" Charlotte had been surprised to hear from Aiden long after their first "date."

"I am doing a lot better hearing your voice, Charlotte. Let's meet up for dinner!"

"Where would you like to go?" Charlotte had been agreeable and open to Aiden's invitation. She had not ruled out the possibility of connecting with Aiden to get to know him. She had wanted to patiently savor her own odd sense of curiosity about Aiden – what had hidden behind those sonorous pleasantries? What kind of man would make so many attempts for a second date? What sort of fellow would call again after one long year?

After a wonderful dinner, Aiden had picked up a guitar left on the small stage in the restaurant bar, and started playing. He had played so naturally and brilliantly that Charlotte had been mesmerized within five minutes! She had found perfection in imperfections -- take Will Ferrell and add an ounce of artistic solemnity, the Frat Pack are transformed mavens. The way Aiden had played music for Charlotte that night had stricken a chord deep inside her. Something innermost had been stirring and answering to his songs. That night, with the emotional stimulation, Aiden had become a virtuoso to Charlotte!

Aiden and Charlotte had been together ever since their second date. They had dated for four years before their marriage. Their courtship had been exhilarating as they had relived the electrifying sensations of knowing each other, falling in love, longing for each other's touch, drifting with the ups-

and-downs of love, and cultivating their shared destiny and purpose.

In young romance, people are still developing their own individualities and may be insulted by their partner's behavior, leading to conflict. In older people's romance, lovers are more matured and prepared to see the way a partner is. It may become a burden on relationships when one must constantly seek one's own worth. Aiden William Melone and Charlotte Lewis Melone were grown enough to have reasonably wholesome self-worth. They were not each other's burden. Rather, they supported each other's pursuits. The conflict in their relationship derived from external factors or forces, mainly form the ways they chose to interact with Aiden's children, Vera and George. Their marriage did not open an easy chapter in their life; it just started another test for them. They had work to do.

34. Conflict Avoider vs. Conflict Resolver

The art of conflict resolution is crucial for building any type of relationships, especially one as intimate as the tie in a marriage. Charlotte Melone was decisive in pursuing her concerns regarding the negative impact her husband's children had on her marriage. Aiden Melone was, quite the opposite, evasive or unresponsive in satisfying the concerns. He turned a blind eye to his own children's impertinently demanding demeanor, hoping everything would just work out itself. Well, it did not and would not.

"Vera and Brandon are visiting, and George is also coming to stay with us. Isn't that great news?!" Aiden was naturally excited about any time the children spent with him

"For how long? Where is George sleeping? We will have to clear out the music room." Charlotte thought about planning right away.

"For several weeks. Yes, we will prepare the music room for George."

So, George stayed in the music room and broke some instruments and chairs, predictably making a mess of the entire house. Vera unsurprising ordered her husband Brandon around, and gave Aiden a long list of tasks to complete for her. Charlotte could not tidy up the house or keep track of their demands fast enough for them to make with more clutters or requests. The children's calls on Aiden and Charlotte were treasured by Aiden, but often turned strenuous for Charlotte.

Charlotte communicated the needs for the children to be more responsible for themselves, in direct manners to her husband and subtle ways to the children. Nothing changed. Aiden was "best-buddy" with his children and the conundrum remained. Charlotte felt further alienated and distanced every time her marriage life was shaped to accommodate the children's wishes.

Aiden was a conflict avoider, which did not create family solidarity. No difficulties were ever alleviated no matter how Charlotte tried. Perhaps avoidance was Aiden's active mode of conflict resolution. While Charlotte asserted the need to resolve her concerns, she was also avoiding contact and thus conflict with Aiden's children. She evaluated her own contradictory responses in hoping Aiden to take the initiative but taking a passive approach herself. She understood the effect her fastidiousness had on her own life with Aiden. Although she had no desire to win any battles, she needed to stand up for herself, not settling for false harmony.

Aiden needed to pay more attention to Charlotte's dilemma in the situation and uphold his relationship with his wife. Ten years into their marriage, Aiden was still stalling for time to process his wrecked marriage with Cina and his complex marriage with Charlotte.

For marriages to work and last, compromising is necessary. You win some, you lose some. The question lies in: what goals can one sacrifice and what must be fulfilled? Can you just play a game to determine who the winner is and let him or her choose the goals in a marriage? Aiden was not willing to compromise his time and energy spent handling his children's issues or reigns over him, while Charlotte tried to balance their life together with managing other people's problems or appetites for attention.

Sometimes Aiden won, and other times Charlotte got to have her ways. More often than not, they both lost.

What then, should a couple do when trying to resolve their conflict? Can they collaborate to attain a win-win situation? How can they address both parties' concerns and needs? The key can be deduced in identifying the underlying concerns, assessing assumptions, and understanding each other's point of view. Would Aiden and Charlotte have enough time of their life to work out their differences? Would they love each other truly to seek solutions fair to both?

"What? My son can't even come staying with us?" Aiden fumed and asked Charlotte.

"It's not that. You've got to teach him to clean up after himself. His words and actions should have consequences." She replied, preparing for his angry bellows.

"That's ridiculous! He should be able to come and go!" Aiden could not see why it's tiring when George was around.

"This is my house, too. Don't you think you need to consider how I feel?" Charlotte pointed out.

"Yes. But he's got to visit us!" Aiden insisted.

"Ok, he's gonna do his own cooking and cleaning." Charlotte made it clear that she would just not toil her body and mind, only to have some spoiled brat acting discourteously toward her.

George, at age of twenty-five, learned that his stepmom was not catering to him again. He cooked for himself and did the dishes sloppily. His father still did his laundry and straightened up after him, but not Charlotte anymore. In a sense, things seemed to improve a little after Aiden and Charlotte set the rules and boundaries.

Aiden rarely expressed his positions about teaching his children or how they should have related to Charlotte; he just let them do whatever they wanted. Charlotte explained why she had come to desire little contact with his children. Her reasons and fears were understood, but her interests and needs, mismatched. Certain degree of intimacy was lost as a result. What would happen if they allowed the situation to stretch into old age? What else could they do to amend their family dynamics? How could they manifest open, healthy conflict so as not to rock the foundation of their marriage?

35. Yes-Sayer vs. Nagger

To have honest communication, Aiden and Charlotte Melone needed to address their differences and value each other's perspectives. Aiden was a yay-sayers who believed in the most exceptional futures for his children, and for all human beings in general. He was a man with immense love, and his love for the world did not go unnoticed. People loved Aiden. Contrarily, Charlotte had a nagging feeling that her life with Aiden was ordinary, consisting of trifling impositions and little gratifying explorations of larger visions in life. She yearned for new knowledge; her desire to travel was insatiable. She wanted to focus her pursuits on her interests in arts, music, and literature. She nagged at Aiden for tailoring his precious life for trivial demands from others. There was so much more they could do with their life together.

"We should go visit Vera and help her and Brandon move to their new house." Aiden suggested.

"I can't take time off work. Frankly if I have time, I'd rather travel somewhere for explorations." Charlotte was being honest about not feeling compelled to go far north to a stepdaughter who was never a stepdaughter in substance. Vera had rejected Charlotte and that was never changed.

Aiden visited Vera and Brandon just to "show up" for them; Charlotte stayed busy and kept on nagging at Aiden. She could not appreciate how every little or not so little chore or undertaking in Vera or

George's life became Aiden's responsibility. She had been self-reliant and independent since the age of eighteen. She had moved and renovated her house, entirely by herself!

Charlotte's nagging was only "nagging" because Aiden never listened. Charlotte's words were inconsequential as Aiden was Aiden, needing to gratify every impulse of his children. Charlotte's needs to spend time doing something more meaningful conflicted with Aiden's need to please his children, or other people. So, they did things to their own likings, often separately, balancing the me-time and the together-time.

Aiden and Charlotte needed to foster "us-against-the-world" mentality, consciously and willingly. Aiden, however, was never against the world; he was operating in a mode more like "us-WITH-the-world. Charlotte let herself off the hook when the "us" concerned Vera and George. Aiden was a yes-sayer, and Charlotte was a nagger – avoiding the difficulties and troubles with Aiden's children, she still could not shake off the guilty feeling of disconnection. When and how could she rid of the shame and remorse of an ordinary life?

36. He Was His Own Person

The thing about Aiden William Melone was that he connected the dots among all people, animals, and things that seemed like mutually exclusive. He had a big heart to tolerate everything, stood his ground, and articulated an aesthetic of life that made sense to himself -- no matter how different or similar Charlotte or others might think or act. He was his own person.

The way Aiden connected with all living and non-living things was, indeed, intriguing. He had the abilities to interest people of all ages and animals of all sorts. Moreover, he linked garage music, high energy rock, folk, jazz, classical, blues, and punk together with fantasy, horror, and sci-fi movies or novels. He was not an erudite, but a jack-of-all-trades. He might not be a sentimental man, but surely, he was a romantic at heart, crying at movies and family reunions numerous times. Aiden was a strong, helpful, and stand-up-straight kind of guy in essence.

What sent Aiden to over drive was the joy he felt when singing the praises of what he considered positive in life. He made a choice for positivity. He felt grateful for what he had in life. He might have a short fuse, but he did not get angry at small things.

"Don't sweat the small stuff. Everything will be fine," said Aiden to Charlotte when she was upset about something he considered insignificant.

"Don't get all bent out of shape just because you can't find the place," said Charlotte to Aiden when he refused to ask for directions, leaving them driving in circles.

What constitutes big things or small things in life, then, is based on one's perceptions and self-identities. Small moments and adjustments in life lead to big things. The decisions Aiden and Charlotte made about their life together deserved better discussions and collaborations. They were two different individuals living a life that comprised dealings with each other's families, outlooks, experiences, worries, fears, hopes, and dreams. They needed to consolidate their circumstances to awaken feelings of togetherness and intimacy that supports a solid, healthy marriage.

37. Music Brought Them Together

There were, from time to time. feelings of warmth and fondness engendered between Charlotte and Aiden's children. Those occasions were created after Aiden urged Charlotte to cease avoiding conflict with the kids and come join their get-togethers. Momentarily they could feel bonded by their civilized and amicable treatment of one another -- until the next hurtful disengagement came along. The evanescent tenderness might be adequate; itmight be all they could create.

"You can play your guitar solo on this one along with my singing and chords." Aiden and George were magnificent jamming together.

"You should bring your Uke and join us." George said to Charlotte when he was happy playing with his dad.

"Yes, I will chime in if I can." Charlotte gladly accepted the invitation.

Music brought them together more often than they cared to admit. They sang and played together. They played "Name the Tune" and had a great time. Aiden named every song, except for the ones produced after the year of 2000, Charlotte named rare pieces no one else knew, usually ballads or folk songs, and George was a huge fan of rock, pop, and EDM. In the end, everyone won, and was drunk with ecstasy and excitement music could stir up in one's soul -- like sudden rays of sunshine in long, cold, and brutal winters that warm up and energize people.

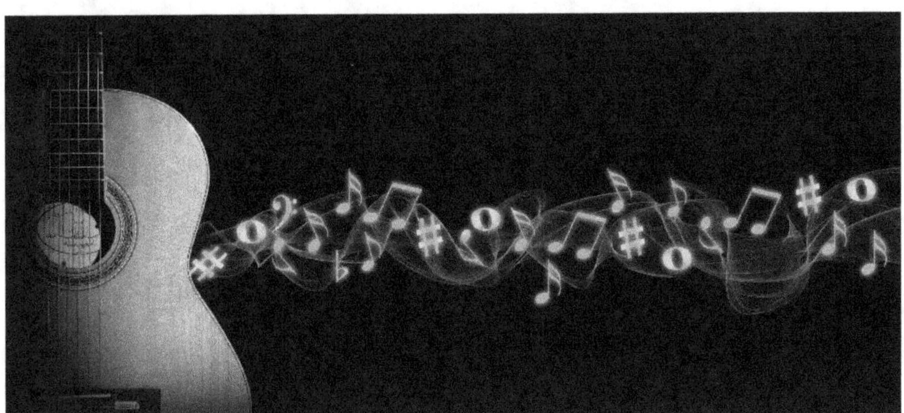

Aiden possessed mysterious abilities to appreciate high arts and low arts, and everything in between. He was both street-smart and book smart. The foundation for his interpretations of the world seemed to have been built upon his rebellion to his own father, his diversion into multiple facets of realities. Music, had always provided an anchor for him, a cradle of inspiration and respite no matter what circumstances life dealt out for him.

38. Birthdays and Holidays Brought Them Together

Another instance where Aiden, Charlotte, and his children felt like a family was when they got together to celebrate birthdays and holidays. Aiden's and Vera's birthdays were only three days apart on the fifteenth and thirteenth of December, around Christmas. Vera often arranged to spend her birthday with her father. The family would drop everything to join them.

"Dad, I found a cheap flight around our birthdays. Brandon and I are flying out to you." Vera called out to Aiden.

"Book the flights then." Aiden always endorsed every suggestion Vera made.

George would pitch in to facilitate his sister's visit, carrying all her presents in his suitcase to attend the soiree at Aiden and Charlotte's house. Charlotte would clean, shop, run errands, and do house chores in a whirlwind, and Aiden would get so excited about Vera and Brandon's visit that he could hardly contain himself. Aiden would ensure that Vera and Brandon had the nicest time and warn everyone else not to make any waves in the mix!

For a moment, Aiden, Charlotte, and his children immersed themselves in the birthday and holiday festivity, all troubles out of mind. They temporarily forgot about their conflict and applied their energy to positive bonding, shopping, eating, drinking, playing, chatting, and -- exchanging presents. Life was good around birthdays and holidays.

The spree might be delightful for some and exhausting for others. But in the end, no one was complaining. They would throw unease or discomfort to the winds. They would enjoy the company of one another. They would match quite a few birthday/holidays wishes and disregard a couple. It seemed that they were all counting their blessings, and there was exceptional jovial atmosphere in the air.

39. Family Reunions Brought Them Together

The Melone family reunions were made of revelries that were on an entirely different scale and level. Once every four years, all of Aiden Melone's relatives would congregate, including siblings, cousins, in-laws, aunts, uncles, grandaunts, granduncles, and their respective household members. Altogether, there were five hundred people gathering at a large event venue to mix and mingle in honor of the Melone clan.

A Melone family reunion lasted for a week, and all the kinsmen set up their living quarters either in tents, RVs, motorhomes, or hotels near the event venue. Large bars, cooking and barbequing facilities, dining halls, music halls, activity halls, speech halls, and outdoor games would be put together for everyone to take part and enjoy. The clan members often felt invigorated, rejoiced, and inspired. Revisiting the family values with their folks was stimulating. Playing, eating, drinking, or simply conversing with people of the same breed was some gratifying experience no other parties could offer. During the day, they would eat, drink, and play games. At night, they would build campfires and sing along with the Melone brothers, the sexy and talented guitarists of the family. The Melones claimed that their relations were so fine that they would befriend the very same people even if they had not been their own family!

Aiden, Charlotte, and his children typically would intermingle with the relatives and appear like a happy troop of four. Aiden would round up Charlotte to greet others. Vera and George would follow their father around. That aroused a sense of unison, an interweaving of different emotions into a single narrative: "We belong with Aiden Melone." The proximity of their physical presences would draw out understandings of one another's thoughts and feelings, their inner selves revealed and discovered.

Vera, though usually aggressive and demanding, would show her bashful side when reciting verses to the entire clan in the speech hall. Her quiet murmurs unveiled a demure girl, blushing with nervousness and apprehension. George, though generally egocentric and pompous, would lend a hand to his younger cousins, nieces, and nephews. His led the batch of young children to play games, giving their parents a chance to have fun. Charlotte was grateful for marrying into the Melone family, while Aiden was elated, jubilant with reminiscences of family anecdotes, his bombastic accounts compelling and remarkably fascinating.

Yes, family reunions brought people together. The love and care laid bare repeatedly moved Aiden

Melone to tears. One by one the Melone family all started bawling, so happy they could die.

40. Equity and Mutual Devotion

With togetherness, there was also parting that followed afterwards. Coming together and slipping away, coming together and slipping-way, coming together and slipping away -- that seemed to be the perpetual cycle the Melone family could not get away from. The relatives would meet and feel like close-knit families; they would then, go about their own lives holding one another in distant memories, until they would meet again next time to get reacquainted. For Aiden Melone, who made phone calls to everyone consistently, it was the memory each get-together created that made meanings for life. His need for human contact never waned.

What faltered was Charlotte's resentment toward her husband, Aiden, or toward Vera and George -- and perhaps Vera's and George's resentment toward Charlotte. In wanting Aiden to be her life companion, Charlotte sought all qualities she defined as a life-long mate in all aspects that Aiden might or might not have control over. Obviously, she needed something that was more fun or profound than resolving conflict with his children or customizing their life to suit his children's demands. Her mentality might have driven her to misinterpret Aiden's needs as the causes of her frustrations or unmet expectations.

"Let's have Vera over for Christmas this year. She and George should take turns," suggested Charlotte.

"Yeah, that'll be wonderful!" Aiden was pleased.

Determined to keep her husband's best interests at heart, Charlotte was more at peace with whatever Aiden did or did not do. She could renounce the irritation she felt about the constant adjustment she made for Aiden's children. But her time and effort had to be applied equally toward making sure that Aiden's and her own needs were fulfilled.

Aiden was not only a life-long mate for Charlotte; he was also a beautiful human being she looked up and devoted herself to. The devotion needed to be mutual. In other words, Aiden and Charlotte needed to work together on every facet of their life, be it conflict resolution, creating fun memories, or seeking purposes of life.

Collaboration fosters respect and trust, which is the foundation of any relationship. Aiden and Charlotte needed to address any conflict or difference openly and truthfully, taking care of each other's needs. Would their marriage thrive? Would it mature? Would they weather the twists and turns, trials and tribulations of life? Would their life together be worthwhile?

41. What of Legacy

Equity or mutual devotion takes time to attain. Both Aiden's and Charlotte's emotions were valid. They needed to hear each other and be heard by each other. The good and bad experiences they went through in their life together could create the space for them to grow. But to reach a point where both felt at ease with all concerns or disparities would be time-consuming. They would have to take time and make the best of their life together, with or without his children. Aiden was a husband, Charlotte's life-long mate, and was also a father. Charlotte was a wife, Aiden's life companion, but would never be close kin to his children.

In time, Aiden picked up more of Charlotte's cues, while Charlotte learned not to be an enemy, a friend, or a relation to his children. She focused on being Aiden's mate, and nothing more.

Charlotte, being Aiden's wife, could not escape being a stepmom to his children, too. For Aiden, it was simpler. He was content with his life while he worked hard, embraced a positive outlook, and had a focus to make himself, his wife, and his children happy. For Charlotte, life implied more than a job or an estate to build to give to someone else. She had a passion for arts, music, literature, and travel. She needed to live a good, creative, and meaningful life. She needed to make an impact or a difference in this world. At the very least, she wanted to write books to fight terrorism, bigotry, or injustice.

Perhaps Aiden's legacy was about the richness of his and his family's lives. Charlotte dreamed of something bigger; she considered it silly to live for small things. What, then, are the small things in life? What are bigger things? If you do a whole bunch of small things, do they add up to "something bigger"?

"You said you don't want to argue about trivial things anymore, remember?" Aiden asked Charlotte.

"That's right! You also promised not to yell anymore." Charlotte reminded Aiden.

"Ok, timeout now. Let's not discuss anymore."

"I'll go for a bike ride. Be back in 10."

The space Aiden and Charlotte created to suspend their disagreement allowed for them to protect each other's internal peace. Keeping calm, they could contemplate what's important to fight for and what needed to be compromised. They got to choose their own priorities and found the middle ground to determine what's most precious for their life together.

Health, love, time, happiness, family, friendship, purpose, knowledge, experience .... -- these were the priceless elements of life for Aiden and Charlotte. Their views of the hierarchy or the make-up of those elements might differ, but their goal was the same: to take control of their life together. Perhaps by saying "yes" to less, Aiden could maintain more of his own sanity. Conceivably Charlotte could also adapt more to the mundane responsibilities.

The smallest things in life amount to the biggest thing. The real mark of greatness is expressed through little actions: kindness, care, compassion, helpfulness, understanding, mercy, and integrity. Aiden and Charlotte might differ in the ways they showed their dignity, but they loved their places in the world all the same. By working together, they might just be able to achieve greater things!

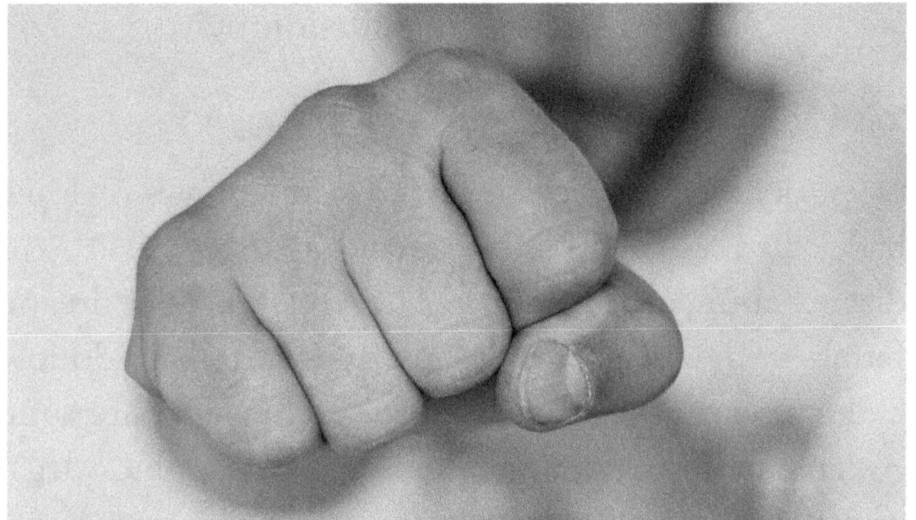

42. She Died of Disillusionment

Before she passed away, Charlotte Lewis Melone had died of disillusionment. She died of disenchantment, of realizing her version of a dream family with an all-loving husband and their doting children would never be her reality. What her life with Aiden had imparted her was a sense of happiness that was not unadulterated with disappointment or imperfection. Then again, what is perfection? Those picture-perfect family portraits always conceal in themselves pains and agonies no outsiders can easily discern. Every family has its own scripture that contains unspoken rules and underlying practices to help its individual members function as a group. Charlotte kept it to herself the mechanisms of dealing with her disappointments and discontents.

And perhaps, that was sufficient for everyone else but Charlotte herself, and so her death was only a self-infliction, a wound that only caused pain to the bearer of the injury, a scar barely noticed by others, hidden somewhere underneath the lovely garments and attires she wore to feel fabulous about life.

Charlotte Melone physically died from the infliction of petty, pesky requests form George! Charlotte did not let herself off the hook enough, to the extent that Aiden's children's constant demand of attention would not become her responsibilities. Charlotte Melone died of a stroke induced by George's car wreck -- one of his many but the biggest in his life.

George Melone had a stroke of luck before the damaging car crash. He earned five thousand a month from a single contract producing music for a label company. The label company owner was deceased before his contract with George matured. His estate paid George fifty-five thousand dollars to honor the contract. With the amount of money he had, George was able to purchase Charlotte's house in the Southwest before she and Aiden moved to the East Coast.

As a first-time homeowner, George was conceited, and his reckless behavior grew even more wild. He loved to test the limits.

"I wanted to see how fast this car can go! Let's race through the highway and meet back in the park," suggested George to his "homies."

"Yep. Let's do it. I bet your baby car can't go as fast as mine!"

Driving at a high speed forty-five miles over the speed limit, George crashed his car into the guardrail over the passing lane. His many phone calls to Aiden woke Aiden and Charlotte up in the middle of the night. He survived the crash, his left arm fractured, and his baby car totaled.

Charlotte did not survive the plague of George's pestilence. While George was in the hospital nursing his arm injury, Aiden had to fly to the Southwest to take care of him, tow his car, deal with the police, and leave Charlotte at home to die of stroke. Home alone without immediate medical attention, Charlotte's sudden death was painless yet tragic. George's stroke of luck ended up giving Charlotte a deadly stroke! In death, she was with Jesus, the conflict, struggle, effort, endeavor, or labor of love in her life, all came to a rest.

43. Time Is the Best Engine

Time may not heal all problems of stepfamilies, bridge differences between men and women, or reduce disparities among rivaling individuals. Time, however, is the best engine that steers people off a miserable path they happen upon or get stuck in. Giving time, destitution will sink in and become a facet of the reality. As time passes, people will seek to free themselves from sufferings one way or another. They will come to terms with their own woes and swallow them with pride, if not free of them. Their copouts will become all too evident to ignore, and their courses of actions, modified, adjusted, and customized to suit the ever-changing tides that are inevitably rocking the ebb and flow of their existences.

Life is not better or worse over time in the grand scheme; life itself is just what it is. The troubles of Aiden Melone's family did not make it a deviant one. The joys and jubilations Aiden and his family experienced together did not signify a superior family, either. Whatever happened was just exactly that, what happened. Individuals' thoughts, opinions, beliefs, actions, conducts, behaviors, manners, and attitudes might have a way that affected how things unfolded. Their story was unique, not lesser or greater, not better or worse for anyone else to judge.

After Charlotte's passing, Aiden Melone acknowledged his own feelings and moved through the grief process at a slow pace, his sorrow and pain intense, and his remorse everlasting. He cried for his loss of his dear wife, Charlotte -- until he could no longer cry, upon his own passing.

44. Sanctity of Forgetting

The English poet, Alexander Pope, is known for a notable proverb: "To err is human; to forgive, divine." It takes an extraordinary person to forgive; the act of forgiving is purely that of a supreme being. People believe that they can forgive for their own peace of mind but will not forget how people have done them wrong to avoid further harm. Is it feasible to forgive, but not forget? Can one truly forgive when keeping all the traumatic memories?

For Aiden Melone and his family, it seemed more viable to remember the lessons learned from their mistakes or the positive emotions they felt on various occasions -- and forget all the hurts and pains their clashes imposed on them or the mishaps occurred in their lives. Aiden would have not been able to live on without forgetting the difficulties that caused Charlotte's stress and sudden death. Charlotte would have not been able to stay married to Aiden without forgetting the problems with his children. Vera and George would have not been able to stay close to their father without forgetting the complications his father's marriage with Charlotte brought to their lives.

Perhaps forgiveness is a prolonged state of forgetting. Perhaps when you consciously intend to forget your ordeals, you can then eliminate the need to forgive. Aiden accepted the flaws in his life. He did not dwell on life's imperfections but seized the blissful state of happiness. He defeated the odd beast of life by forgetting. He was able to build a good life. Indeed, there is sanctity in forgetting.

45. A Life Larger than Life

Aiden William Melone was a stellar salesman whose aura encompassed personas of a stately man, an athlete, a jack-of-all trades, a good fellow, and a soulful musician -- not the bad-boy type that would consume you, but the make of a protector to be trusted with all your troubles and problems. He brought out the best in people. He was a natural leader, with the stature and flair of a trailblazer for life's better paths, the sort legends are made of.

Aiden William Melone was a charming, self-made man. He dedicated his whole life to honest, caring, and stimulating human interactions. He was successful as a businessman and enjoyed a creative life. He was extraordinarily vivacious around people, but never gave in to the conformist pressures that would deny a rightly satisfying and fulfilled life.

In his animated incessant talks, Aiden carved out his destiny with gusto and zest. What he came to understand was the need to reciprocate the depth of his wife's love. He had his share of vulnerability and flaws. His life with Charlotte rose above the ordinary with progressive awareness of intimacy that required patience, consideration, empathy, and collaboration.

Aiden realized that his ambition, aspiration, and association with people, with the world, was supported by the strong foothold built by his loved ones. He lived his life brilliantly with gratitude. He ate; he drank; he made merry. He had an interesting life that was not at all perfect, but adjusted, developed, changed, learned, and well thought out.

Aiden celebrated the human spirit. He was ageless as he was a kind, warm, bright, pleasant, and light-hearted person who made others laugh, think, and discover themselves. He was capable of tongue-in-cheek humor, but was also dead serious about things that mattered. He was a delight to be around, notable, and memorable. He was a man with immense love – his life, a life larger-than-life.

Thank you for reading!

Dear Reader,

I hope you enjoyed *A Man with Immense Love.* I must tell you that I have grown as a person in writing about the protagonist and other characters in this novel. Indeed, writing is a medicine and learning process for me, and I hope reading it too, helps you somehow, escape, cope, or acquire new skills and tools in living your own life.

All the characters mentioned here in the book, true or imaginative, have contributed to the world I construct, and have their own voices. I created them with the purpose of illustrating a way of living life that hopefully can be more peaceful or more manageable.

The intricacies of human relationships are often challenging; human interactions, especially among members of stepfamilies, can be daunting, to say the least. It is always through genuine self-reflection and self-education, our relationships can survive, weather storms, and succeed in thriving to a higher level. And we humans, in turn, can see the brighter side of many aspects of life, and grow to be happier, healthier people. A glimpse of light, of hope, is what I trust for you, readers.

Finally, I need to ask a favor. If you are so inclined, I'd love a review of *A Man with Immense Love.* Your honest review is the most precious feedback I could have. Please find below a link to my author page on Amazon:

http://amazon.com/author/aliciasulozeron

Other platforms where you could communicate your thoughts about my book are as follows:

https://www.linkedin.com/in/alicia-su-lozeron
http://www.aacs.website/en/membership/featured
http://www.aliciasulozeron.com/

Please make yourself heard by voicing your opinions. Thank you so much again for reading *A Man with Immense Love.* I look forward to reading your review.

Sincerely,

Alicia Su Lozeron

A Man with Immense Love

Author: Alicia Su Lozeron

About the Author

Asia-Literacy and Global Competence Mentor |
Founder of AACS | Author | Interpreter/Translator
Licensed English Language Arts Teacher

Think Global Live Noble

Alicia Su Lozeron is the author of numerous news/magazine articles and short stories. She holds a Master's degree in English and Comparative Literature from Columbia University in the City of New York, and is licensed as a secondary-school English Language Arts teacher in NV, CA,

MI, PA, TX and AZ. Through her writing career as well as the communication management/consulting company she founded, Asia-America Connection Society, she aims to raises awareness about global competence, and to connect the West to the significant economic and cultural contributions the Asian segment offers.

Alicia Su Lozeron's collections of articles and vignettes in *Asia-Literacy and Global Competence* (2017) and *Global Competence Revisited* (2019) highlight her musings of cultural interactions; they layout the groundwork for her many endeavors. *Writings in the Time of Coronavirus* (2021) continues to observe and call for human justices and upstanding values. Her debut novel, *The Un-death of Me* (2016), depicts a world traveler and immigrant Asian American woman's life in a fresh light. It is a fictional world full of contemporary and global resonance; it is about many subjects: alienation, individuality, self-doubt, self-discovery, complexities of love and marriage, quests of fulfillment, happiness, justice, and cultural diversity, to reduce discrimination, and mankind's bias or prejudice. *A Man with Immense Love* (2022) moves forward to advance musings of humanity issues. It is a prayer for a larger life, an understanding of human conditions, and a realization of human complexities or gray areas of life; it is full of possibilities for human compassion and kindness. Through the honest and generous protagonist, Aiden William Melone, the author reveals how a human mind could be obtuse and alert at the same time – how a good soul is the key to happiness. The story is subtly exposing of human flaws but immeasurably uplifting. It implies that we humans can build a healthier life, starting with a good thought, a kind intent, and then developing a wholesome mindset that is capable of evolving, growing and attaining meanings in our humble existences.

Alicia Su Lozeron
Asia-America Connection Society
Think Global Live Noble
Phone 702-505-9506
E-mail aliciasulozeron@gmail.com; info@aacs.website

What readers see -- Alicia Su Lozeron's work:

• helps me overcome difficulties or fears and find beauty in positive human interactions;
• helps me appreciate people of various backgrounds, and expand knowledge about the world;
• helps me better interracial or blended family relations;
• helps me savor intricate feelings and emotions about important subjects in life;
• helps me gain enjoyment through poetic narrations;
• helps me heighten a new perspective of hope, courage, and respect for others;
• helps me raise awareness about cultural competence;
• helps me nurture a well-rounded outlook;
• motivates me to promote an open/just community;

• urges me to develop ability to see the big picture using multiple frames of references;
• helps me strengthen the ability to express genuine love;
• helps me decrease conflict by learning to trust and resolve disagreements….

Detailed Information:
https://www.linkedin.com/in/alicia-su-lozeron
http://www.aliciasulozeron.com
http://amazon.com/author/aliciasulozeron
http://www.aacs.website/en/services/authors-and-books
https://www.facebook.com/aliciasulozeron